FOREVER IMMORTAL

AMELIA HUTCHINS

FOREVER IMMORTAL

Authored By: Amelia Hutchins
Copy edited by: E & F Indie Services
Edited by: E & F Indie Services
Published in (United States of America)
10 9 8 7 6 5 4 3 2 1

ALSO BY AMELIA HUTCHINS

UPCOMING SERIES

<u>Wicked Knights</u>
Oh, Holy Knight
If She's Wicked 2019

<u>A Crown of Ashes</u>
Coming Soon

WARNING!

Warning: This book is **dark**. It's **sexy**, hot, and **intense**. The author is human, you are as well. Is the book perfect? It's as perfect as I could make it. Are there mistakes? Probably, then again, even **New York Times top published** books have minimal mistakes because like me, they have **human editors**. There are words in this book that won't be found in the standard dictionary, because they were created to set the stage for a paranormal-urban fantasy world. Words such as 'sift', 'glamoured', and 'apparate' are common in paranormal books and give better description to the action in the

Warning! (Cont'd)

story than can be found in standard dictionaries. They are intentional and not mistakes.

About the hero: chances are you may **not** fall instantly in **love** with him, that's because **I don't write men you instantly love**; you grow to love them. I don't believe in **instant-love**. I write flawed, raw, caveman-like **assholes** that eventually let you see their redeeming qualities. They are **aggressive, assholes**, one step above a caveman when we meet them. You may *not* even like him by the time you finish this book, but I promise you will **love** him by the end of this **series**.

About the heroine: There is a chance, that you might think she's a bit naïve or weak, but then again who starts out as a badass? Badasses are a product of growth and I am going to put her through **hell**, and you get to watch **her** come up **swinging** every time I knock her on her ass. That's just how I do things. How she reacts to the set of circumstances she is put through, may not be how you as the reader, or I as the author would react to that same situation. Everyone reacts differently to circumstances and how Ciara responds to her challenges, is how I see her as a character and as a person.

I don't write love stories: I write fast paced, knock you on your ass, make you sit on the edge of your seat wondering what happens in the next kind of books. If you're looking for cookie cutter romance, this isn't for you. If you can't handle the ride, ***un-buckle your seatbelt and get out of the roller-coaster car now***. **If not, you've been warned.** If nothing outlined above bothers you, carry on and **enjoy the ride!**

FOREVER IMMORTAL

FOREVER IMMORTAL

CHAPTER ONE

Graves spread farther than the eye could see, expanding across the long-forgotten meadow in Scotland. I placed the flowers on the smooth marble headstone that I'd purchased last week after I'd discovered this one had been cracked. These were the fallen ones, the hunters who had lost their lives fighting against immortals. I lifted my eyes, studying the storm that was rolling in from the ocean, the salt in the air an indication of something more sinister brewing.

I took in the rows of numbered markers, knowing that one day, mine would be among them. It was just fact, the knowledge that someday soon, my card would be plucked and my fate sealed. Hunters didn't live long, but then we fought against immortals that had a huge advantage over us. I started back towards the cemetery's entrance, noting the man who watched me with a knowing look in his dull brown gaze. His hand held a brown paper bag; the familiar scent of alcohol hit my nose as I slowed to take him in.

"You planning to drink yourself stupid?" I asked as

I stopped in front of him.

"Is that an option?" he laughed as he sat on the hood of my car, staring out over the silent cemetery. "I still don't understand why you come here so often."

"My parents are in there, somewhere," I said as I took the bottle from him, tipping it up as the alcohol burned its way through my system. "Is this vodka or piss?" I sputtered as I handed it back to him.

Jesse was like me, orphaned and alone in the world. We'd grown up together, killed our first creatures together, and lived together in a shitty little apartment away from campus. Others preferred the hunters' campus—safety in numbers, they claimed—but I didn't agree. To me, it seemed stupid to be one big target for our enemies, all living under one roof.

"Mine too, Isa," he said as he took a swig and pointed to an older section of the sprawling cemetery, which held retired hunters who had been brought back to bury here. Not that many had, since the average lifespan for hunters was fortyish. "Do you think we will end up in one of these nameless, depressing graves?"

"Maybe, maybe not. I mean, we could be the lucky ones," I shrugged his words off. Unlike him, I wasn't human, not entirely. I was a half-breed. Part-siren, part-human, and all fucked up.

"You think that siren inside of you will save us?" he chuckled.

"No, no, I think she is dormant and doesn't help me out, ever. That is what they prefer, though, so that is what I am."

"I wish I had something else inside of me," he admitted.

"Yeah, because being a freak is so cool?" I scoffed as I pushed my thick silver hair away from my face and stared out over the silence of the night. Lifting my emerald-green eyes to the angry clouds, I inhaled the heather and salt of the Highlands as I poked the creature inside of me.

My mother had been a full-blooded siren, one of the last in existence. Drake, the headmaster and elder of our faction of hunters, had told me the story a hundred times. My mother, the queen of sirens, had been attacked and left for dead when they'd found her and brought her to the compound. My father's lifeless body had been beside her, as if he'd tried to defend her, and yet failed. They tried to save her, but had failed, and yet I'd been born and accepted as one of their own. But there were rules because of what I was. I was a monster, one they used and feared, but with enough medication, my siren slept within me.

"We should go," he said, and I nodded as I watched him walk to the nearest garbage can to drop the empty bottle into it. "I'll drive," he announced.

"I don't think so," I uttered beneath my breath as I studied his wide shoulders. He seemed off tonight, more distant than usual. "You drank an entire bottle of vodka. I'd hate to be the only hunters who ever died in a car crash," I said with a pointed look. He tossed the keys into the air, and I snatched them up as I smirked at him.

I had just pulled on to the country road when my phone buzzed, and I eyed the message that had an address and three marks on it, indicating there were three vampires assumed to be at the address. My eyes moved to Jesse, who shook his head.

"I'm drunk, Isa," he muttered as he watched me carefully.

"I'm not," I returned as I pushed my foot to the gas pedal and started towards the location. "You can wait in the car."

"Why do I get the feeling I'm going to have to save your ass, drunk?"

"When have I ever needed to be saved?" I scoffed as I handed him my phone, knowing he'd push the address into the GPS which would signal the other hunters in the area that we were en route to the location.

"That one time when your leather pants were too tight, and you got covered in blood. You needed help to get out of them then, remember?"

"Yes, you saved me from the scary leather pants," I snorted as I eyed the map on my phone and then stared at the barn that sat on the hilltop. "What the hell?" I asked as I pulled over and pushed the location again before restarting it.

"I think that is the location." He stared at it as we sat there, studying the area before I opened the car door and climbed out. It took him a moment to even move, as if he was worried about something, but eventually, he poured out of the car and stretched.

"Are you staying with the car?" I asked.

"Tempting, but even drunk, I can help."

"If you slow me down, Jesse, I'll kick your ass," I smirked as he rolled his eyes dramatically.

I opened the trunk, pulling out stakes and holy water, and pushed them into the strap I wore that crossed over my chest. Normally, they would have a team here already. It was too quiet, and the longer I stared at the barn, the worse the sensation of being watched grew.

"Are you thinking what I'm thinking?" he asked as he studied the woods around us.

"If you're thinking that this is off, then the answer is yes. I don't see a surveillance team or anyone else."

"It's all wrong, buttercup," he laughed as he pulled out a jug of holy water and doused himself in it. I frowned at his abuse of the water, which wasn't easy to come by. More and more, churches stopped making it, and our own priest had grown lazy.

I closed the trunk and started to walk around it, studying the land around the barn. It wasn't a normal hive if, in fact, it even was one. There was nowhere to run here, no shade for the vampires to escape to if they were discovered in the daylight hours.

"I don't like this," he growled as he closed the distance to my side. "Get back in the car, Isa."

"If we don't do it, someone else will be sent out to handle it; we don't run," I muttered as I frowned, continuing to note the details and lack thereof. Pulling out my phone, I looked at the number that had sent the location, and the crease in my brow furrowed as I noted the number wasn't one of ours.

"Isa…" Jesse said as power slithered around us. "Run!" he screamed as the air around us grew thick with it. I turned, starting to do as he'd said as I watched something slam into him. I screamed, letting the siren out as everything inside of me snapped. I reached down, pulling Jesse up with me as I started towards the woods to find cover.

Branches slapped my arms and my face, stinging them as I looked over at Jesse, who held his stomach.

He had a massive wound across it, and the blood that poured from it would make it near impossible to hide from the vampires hunting us. He was living fucking bait.

We stumbled at the creek's edge, and I pushed him into the water as I turned, staring at the area around it. I could feel them, and the siren, that naughty bitch, was purring to fight as she lifted within me, watching the shadows. She was driven by sex, the need to lure men into her web and capture them. I frowned as the silence stretched out, stakes in both hands as I surveyed the woods around us. I knelt down beside Jesse, who had gone silent even with the gaping wound in his stomach.

"I'm a lost cause, you need to run, buttercup."

"Fuck that," I snapped as I set the stakes down, pulling out the holy water to cover his wound in as he sat in the ice-cold creek. "Friends don't leave friends to be vamp snacks. Remember, no asshole left behind."

"Now isn't that cute, the wee one thinks she can save 'im," a deep voice whispered behind me.

I spun around, letting the siren take center stage as I smiled coldly at the vampire. His eyes slowly settled over me, striking brown, amber eyes that made mine look dull in comparison. My hand wrapped around the stake as I rose to face him.

"She's a wee thing, but I bet she bites, the best ones always do," he laughed as I took in his dark black hair and the curve of his lips. He was beautiful in a rugged way, but then most of the undead were.

"I bet she screams when she rides a cock," another one hissed.

"If you leave now, I'll let you live."

"Beg me tae live, lass," the third one said as he stared past me to where Jesse was watching us.

I opened my mouth, letting the siren hiss at them as the tallest one tilted his head, studying me. He didn't move, not even as the others tried to get closer to me. I felt him poking against my mind as he tried to grasp what I was, or what I would do. Those sinfully amber eyes narrowed as he looked past where I stood and down at Jesse, who held his stomach as he lay still, knowing the siren was in full control.

"Touch me," I begged, the song of my words coming out in layers as I lured them to their deaths.

"Tempting, but I will pass, siren. Ye have something that belongs tae me, and I want her back. Ye will be my leverage. Ye and ye poor wee boyfriend,"

"I'm not wee, asshole," Jesse snapped as my hair began to float against the wind and my skin glowed.

"Touch me, and I will pleasure you, vampire."

"I said nae, wench. I ken what ye are, and ye are nae even tempting tae the monster within me."

Ouch.

My siren recoiled from the barb, offended that he'd been able to withstand the trance she had tried to lure him into. Hands touched me, and I swallowed as the other vampires did as I had asked, along with Jesse. Well fiddlesticks.

"Stop that," I urged as I slapped at hands as the other vampire watched his friends and mine trying to gain my attention. "Stop!" I screamed and watched as they paused, doing as my voice had instructed.

"A newly born siren," he scoffed as he blinked in and out of my vision before something crashed against my head. Darkness took hold as arms caught me, my vision blurring as I stared into the smiling lips of the vampire. "You're goona be fun tae break, wee one."

CHAPTER TWO

Water splashed into my face, and I lifted my eyes, taking in the rope that had been wrapped around my hands and attached to a hook. Below me was a metal bin, a way for them to catch any blood loss from their victim. I turned my head, staring at Jesse, who had yet to wake. In front of me, the dreamy-eyed guy watched me. I looked beyond him, searching for the exits to get my bearings. This wasn't my first rodeo of being captured, and I intended to make damn sure it wasn't my last. My vision swam as I groaned against the pain in my head. Where the hell was the siren when I needed her? She was all for being present when the fun part played out, but the moment I was in trouble, she vanished.

"Ye are a wee thing, are nae ye?" he chuckled as he moved closer, letting his finger trail over my naked torso. "Nae much o' a hunter, now are ye?"

"Hey, asshole, you want to get to second base, you best buy me dinner first."

"Oh, wee one, ye *are* my dinner," he chuckled

darkly as he watched me test the ropes.

"Is that so? Mmm, I don't think you will like how I taste. I've been told that I am bitter."

"I bet ye taste like heaven, siren," he growled as he let his hand move up to my face, cupping my cheek as I pulled away.

"Get to the fun stuff already."

"The part where I drain ye, or the part where I tell ye why I 'ave nae killed ye yet?"

"I prefer neither, to be honest; it's not you, it's me. Fangs are a hard limit for me," I laughed huskily, sensing the siren as she raised her head, peering out at the male before us. Now she wanted to come out and play? The bitch was bipolar and had one freaking need. Well, maybe two. To fuck, and to kill.

"Hello, pretty," he uttered as he stared at me through gold-flecked eyes. "And here they said ye were all but extinct."

"Did they?" I asked. "Probably because you and your kind hunted us down for sport," I hissed.

"Nae, ye doona get tae blame that on us, wee one. Ye slaughtered human men that would nae stay with ye, and so ye murdered the poor men. Ye brought it upon yourselves."

"Why don't you come closer and I'll show you why men enjoy us," I said huskily, letting the siren within enter my voice. "I bet you picked up some tricks in your old age, didn't you?"

"Tempting, lass," he smirked. "But ye are nae even me type. I prefer my lasses with oot sass."

"Isa?" Jesse groaned, and I turned, eyeing him as he came to. "Fuck, my stomach aches, and my mouth taste like ass."

"That's blood coursing through ye, mon. My blood tae be exact."

I frowned as Jesse's eyes went wide with horror. My graze dropped to the healed wound in his stomach and nausea rolled through my stomach. His head turned, and he stared at me. I knew what was running through his mind, because it was pounding in mine, too.

"No," he whispered.

"Nae, nae yet," the vampire said. "But I'm a hybrid vampire. I am born, which means ye will change with the simple drop I gave ye, or die if ye choose nae tae feed. That choice is yours."

My eyes closed as I exhaled slowly, fighting for strength to endure what would come if Jesse changed into one of them. I heard the emotion in his voice as he said my name over and over again. Slowly, I opened my eyes and turned, staring at him as the blood pounded in my ears.

"No, Isa, he's lying. You and me, forever, remember?" he pleaded.

"Isn't that cute?" the vampire crooned as he closed the distance between us and bit into his wrist. I turned, staring at him as his eyes turned golden and my pulse jumped. Jesus H. Christ, he really was a fucking hybrid? "It's your turn, wee bonnie lass," he uttered.

I closed my mouth, begging the siren to fight with me, and yet she did nothing. I felt her with me, the calmness of her, as if she was growing bored with what was happening. His warm flesh touched against my lips, and I shook my head, fighting against it as his body pressed against mine. His free hand pushed against my jaw, forcing it open as the copper taste of him touched against my tongue. Instead of fighting it, I bit into his flesh, flashing emerald eyes as I sucked him in. His own eyes lit from within, as if his own monster was watching me.

His hand that held my jaw released it, and something bellowed beside us as I drank deeply, sucking it down my throat as he watched me. I wanted to climb him, and sink him into my flesh. He was addictive. The taste of him against my taste buds exploded as I moaned around his flesh.

"Jesus, she's a beast," someone else muttered.

The vampire I fed from pushed my hair away from my eyes, watching me with a look of pure lust in his golden hybrid eyes until he pulled his arm away.

"Isadora MacPherson, you look at me!" Jesse screamed, and I turned, staring at him with blood dripping down my chin. I groaned as my eyes swung back to the vampire I craved.

"More," I hissed as I licked my lips, and a sinful smile flitted over his lips as his stare grew heavy with lust.

"Dayum, I want one," the other vampire muttered, and my eyes moved to him, staring at him briefly before my gaze dropped to his frame and then slowly moved back to the vampire I'd tasted.

"Nae, ye doona want one o' them," he growled.

"Cian, I want one. Look at her," he crooned as he stepped forward. "She's fucking beautiful."

"She's a fucking siren," he growled harshly, and the other vampire stopped mid-step.

"You're fucking kidding, mon. She can nae be,

they're all but gone."

"Oh, the wee thing is definitely one. Ye smell that? That is her essence, luring us in. Everything aboot that creature is created tae bring men down tae theirs knees at her dainty wee feet. With nary a whisper o' a word, she can destroy a man."

"Isadora, look at me. Push her away," Jesse begged.

"Nae, let the wee thing oot tae play," Cian said. "I like her more," he uttered as his friend brought over an assortment of knives laid out on a metal tray.

"Use me," Jesse snapped.

"Play with me," I begged in a husky tone. "Come play with me."

Cian's mouth curved into a knowing smile as his golden eyes lifted to hold mine. He uttered words to the man who continued to unveil his torture table, and yet the only thing the siren processed was his power, his blood that coursed through her as he stood just out of reach. I watched as he lifted the shirt over his head to reveal thick coils of muscle and tattoos that littered his chest and arms as he turned back, watching me through hooded eyes.

"I'm ready tae play with ye, siren."

No one paid attention to Jesse, who was screaming as he fought against the ropes that held him. The siren turned my head, staring at the tray of instruments he planned to use for torture before my lip curved into a smile. I felt her pulling back and screamed as I shivered with the change; the subtle exit of her sent a shock through my body, and I shivered violently as a moan expelled from my throat.

"That's nae normal, is it?" the other vamp asked as

he took in my emerald-green eyes.

"Nae, she's a half-breed." Cian stepped forward, his hand rose to touch my cheek, and I pulled away. My eyes burned with rage as I tasted the blood in my mouth and I kicked out, nailing him on the shin, which was way off from where I had aimed for, but blood was coursing through me, ancient, powerful blood that intensified everything. "Meet the real wee Isa," he laughed huskily.

"Nae, I liked the other one. This one seems almost human, aye?" He scoffed.

"Almost, but nae immune tae my blood," Cian said, staring at me with a dark look that terrified me, and made the siren perk up and take notice. Bipolar bitch needed to pick a side, and hopefully, she chose mine since she was a part of me. "We're tae the fun stuff, Isa."

"My name is Isadora, asshole. My friends call me Isa, and you and me? We're not there yet, sweetheart."

"Your siren enjoys me; maybe I'll take her fer a ride later? I bet she lets me play with ye and more, aye?"

"She doesn't want your dick, asshole. She wants to rip out your throat. Besides, she's bipolar at best, and nasty when she's pissed off." I watched him through narrow eyes as he reached for a blade and stepped in front of me.

"I like it rough, ye ken? I actually prefer it that way. We're going tae play a game. I'm going tae carve ye up, and the boy is going tae watch me. If he answers me truthfully, ye won't feel as much pain. If he lies, I take a piece of ye, and ye get tae live with what is left."

"Sounds kinky," I uttered as I turned to look at Jesse with a sad smile. "Remember that time I kissed your girlfriend, and she dumped you because I kissed better?" I asked.

"Isa…"

"I'm going to need you to go back to that day and remember how pissed off you were."

"You said the siren kissed her," he frowned.

"No, all me," I replied as I watched the vampire moving closer. "I knew she was shallow, so I made out with her. I knew you'd find out, and you did. It was better you be mad at me than find out she'd slept with half the football team and the cheerleaders," I babbled as my nerves started to tense.

"The football team *and* the cheerleaders? Damn, I thought she looked exhausted."

I laughed as I turned to look at him. "She was," I busted out laughing as he watched me.

"Isa, you're evil, but I love you," he uttered as he swallowed hard.

"I know," I stated. "I'm going to need you not to give this asshole what he wants."

"I won't," he said as he closed his eyes and then turned away, staring up at the ceiling as the knife skimmed over my flesh.

"Ye two are cute, how long ye been fucking one another?" Cian asked as I stared at the blade that kissed my flesh.

"I'm a virgin," I smirked as I lifted my eyes to his.

"I can teste that theory if ye want," he laughed huskily as he dragged the blunt edge of the blade over my flesh.

The blade stopped, and I lifted my eyes to his, unwilling to watch as it pushed through my flesh. I felt it cut through it, pushing through the split between my ribs as a scream bubbled in my lungs. I refused to make a noise; at least, I refused until my mouth opened and I hissed until it rushed out as a scream of pain.

"Hunters broke into a warehouse and took a female, where is she?" he asked.

"I don't know," Jesse said and the blade twisted as a whimper escaped my lips.

"Wrong answer," he hissed as he pulled the blade out and pushed into a new spot, missing every organ with precision as he pressed it deeper. I screamed as sweat beaded against my brow, the dripping of my blood running down my naked torso and over the thin panties I wore. Dripping against the metal tin that collected it. "I won't ask ye again, ye understand? I will carve her flesh and feed it tae ye."

"You think we get told dick? We are nothing but the ones they send out to die, asshole. I cannot tell you, because I don't fucking know. This wasn't the plan, you never fucking…"

"Silence, boy. Tsk, tsk," his tongue clicked against his teeth as he bent over, licking a trail of my blood up to the knife. He twisted it as his eyes narrowed and his hand stilled. I whimpered as his eyes widened as he stared at me, even as I began to cave to the pain that took me into the black velvet of nothingness. "Fucking hell," he snapped harshly. "Ye taste like sin."

CHAPTER THREE

Cian

I watched the female, her pale skin smooth as the crimson blood dripped from the wound, sliding over the creamy white flesh until it dripped into the pan at her feet. She was utter perfection. Silver hair clung from her back in soft curls, emerald eyes focused, only to lose it with the pain I delivered. Her red lips opened as screams and moans escaped even as she tried to silence them.

If they didn't have my sister, I'd have enjoyed playing a more subtle game of cat and mouse with her, but this was fucking war. Adelaide was the sixth female to go missing from my kingdom, and I was tired of them thinking we wouldn't fight back.

My tongue ached to taste her blood again, to watch as she fed from mine. I hadn't expected that, and at my age, it was hard to shock me. A siren hidden among hunters, now that was something you didn't see every day either. Even more shocking was her emerald eyes, which belonged to an ancient order of sirens who ruled and coveted power.

"She's in and oot," I growled as I turned, staring at the boy she'd joked with in the moments before being tortured.

"Leave her alone," he begged.

"Tell me what ye ken aboot the women the hunters are taking and I will. Ye have my word." I watched him as he shook his head.

"I honestly don't know dick about any women. We don't take prisoners. We kill them all, no mercy. I didn't do it, and neither did she. You know that already, so what the fuck is this?"

"Ye ken ye should lie tae me aboot that, aye?" I snapped. "And I never promised tae be gentle or kind, nae did I?"

"Would you spare her life if I did?" he asked as my eyes narrowed.

"Ye love her," I laughed wickedly.

"Since the moment she broke Bobby's nose for calling me a sissy. She was five."

"Pussy," Lars laughed.

"He was ten, I was four, and he was three times our size."

"Ouch," I laughed as I turned, studying the blood that ran down her scantily-clad body. She was strong-minded, but then as a siren, she'd have to be to gain any control over it. Her breasts weren't large but enough to fit in my hands perfectly. Her thin hips were tattooed with pink bows on them that sat just above her panties, something that drew the eye, and yet I could taste her pureness in her blood.

She hadn't lied; she was a virgin, and how she'd contained the siren was curious. There was an addiction in her blood; the call to feed from her was addictive. Fucking hunters and their messing with creatures they didn't understand, they made her suppress her inner beast. When she finally let loose the hold she held, she'd fuck her way into next year, and my inner wolf preened at the idea of being the one she rode.

"Your father comes, aye?"

"Nae, he's oot fer the week. He's hunting down leads on the women. More went missing last week in the lowlands, and now the entire clan is coming tae find them. Fer now, we focus on that warehouse."

I knew the boy listened to every word, hung on them as if he thought he was escaping this dungeon that held him without some punishment. He wouldn't be leaving here mortal, and his own kind would hunt him down for what he was, but I'd received an offer too good to pass up on. I'd be damn sure whatever the two shared was severed to teach him that deals with the devil had consequences.

"Bring in the lass," I ordered as I turned, staring at the boy who stared at the siren, unknowingly drawn to the sweet flesh that oozed her pheromones to any male close enough to smell them. Shit was heady, alluring, and deadly. It was a good thing I was immune, or I'd be so deep in her that they would never find me again with the scent her flesh was giving off.

My eyes swung back to the female who rolled her head, emerald-green eyes ablaze with pain as she inhaled and whimpered. Fuck if my cock didn't respond to the sweetness of her noises as I watched her coming alert to her predicament. Her lips parted as I stepped closer, dragging my index finger over those full, soft lips.

"There's me wee bonnie lass," I uttered as I pushed my finger into the heat of her mouth, watching as she blinked. I withdrew it the moment her teeth crashed together to snap it off. "Ye like tae bite? I like tae bite too," I growled as I moved closer, pressing my muscles against the soft curves of her body as I threaded my fingers through her hair, exposing the sweet curve of her neck. My tongue slid over her weak pulse as I let the incisors push from my gums. The moment I pushed against her neck, she moaned as if I'd entered her sweet cunt.

Her body responded instantly, and hell if mine didn't ignite with excitement at the arousal that slid between her thighs. She whimpered as I drank from her, sucking her life essence into my veins. She tasted of heaven and sex, her sweet noises increasing as I took more from her, slowly pulling away to watch her blood slide down her firm breast before I leaned over, flicking my tongue against the wound before cleaning the mess she'd made.

My hybrid senses pulsed, sensing the wrongness of her as color brightened and my heart thudded, beating faster as I pulled back, staring at her with the knowledge that her blood tasted different from others, and it wasn't the siren within that created it. My mind refused to acknowledge what my blooded heart felt. It didn't matter what my body did, or how it reacted. She was a hunter, bred to hunt down and murder my kind. That was just fucking fine with me, because I'd been created to face her kind head-on. So what the fuck was the universe thinking with this sick joke?

I wasn't known for having mercy either, and I enjoyed playing with my food. Her eyes opened and her mouth moved, but no words escaped past her lips. Her blood coated my flesh, ran through my veins, and I felt her arousal as she hung there, helpless to do aught but what I allowed her to.

"Sweet girl," I crooned as I moved closer, kissing her lips as my fangs scraped over her delicate lip, letting her taste her own blood as she moaned against me. Fuck, she was addicting to taste. Her arousal made my balls twinge, and worse, the more noises she made, the more my cock stood to attention. "Wake up; it's time tae play with me." My voice was thick, husky from the taste of her blood mixed with the scent of her sweet flesh.

"No," she hissed. "Didn't even buy me dinner first, you dick," she uttered through bloodied lips swollen from the slice I'd placed there. My hand loosened against her hair as I licked the wound, closing it. A smile tugged against my lips as her words registered.

"I told ye, ye are my dinner, lass. Yer pussy is wet fer me," I pointed out crudely, watching as she lifted her eyes to mine, studying them as she realized she was in control, and that her cunt wept to be fucked still, even though her siren had burrowed into her. Everything that was masculine inside of me growled at her reaction to me. "It's all ye, she has nae even peeked through those bonnie green eyes o' yours."

"Mmm, well that sucks."

I smiled at her reply, watching her pupils dilate as her body ached to be filled by more than my fangs. She may have hated me and my kind, but fuck if her body didn't respond to me. I'd expected the siren to come out and play, yet she hadn't. They were connected, and yet something pushed her deep into the human mind this wee girl controlled.

"Kiss me," I ordered, pressing my lips against hers, expecting her to do as I commanded, and instead, she pulled her mouth away and closed her pretty green eyes. "I said, kiss me," I demanded as my voice came out layered, the command enough to make any human mind do as I bid them to. She gasped as she leaned forward, slowly touching her lips against mine as I waited for her to deepen it.

The moment they touched against mine, lingering, her sweet tongue slipped free, tracing my bottom lip as a moan expelled from her lungs. "Go to hell, asshole."

I stepped back, staring at her as my eyes narrowed at the huskiness of her words, and yet she had the ability to tell me off. The door behind us cracked open as Lars entered through it. She was strong of mind, too strong. She'd been trained to suppress her siren, medication more than likely, but that alone wouldn't have held it at bay. No, her body was a temple, one she had wielded like a weapon. Knicks covered the flesh of her torso, but those were from various fights. I walked around her, noting the slices at the back of her calves, and anger pulsed through me. They'd made damn sure she contained the beast within her, abusing her until she'd learned to hide it.

"What do ye want done with this one?" Lars asked as he held the feeder's hand.

"Slice her throat and give her tae him. She betrayed us tae hunters, her death is owed tae the clan."

I watched as the absent-minded female followed

Lars as he moved next to Jesse, slicing through the neck of the feeder as he pressed his mouth to her neck, holding her severed throat against his mouth. The boy denied the hunger, at first, the indecision playing out in his eyes giving me hope he'd survive in his new form.

Hunters evolved, but then so did we, to be able to withstand the never-ending onslaught of them that hunted us down, regardless of how careful we were. No creature was safe from them, and we'd joined forces with the werewolves, creating a new breed we had kept hidden for centuries. We had created hybrids, which could walk in both worlds, bred for one purpose: hunting our enemies to protect our people.

"No," she whispered as she watched him with tears falling from her eyes. "No! Jesse, look at me, stop!" she wailed as she struggled against the ropes that bound her hands to the chain above her head. She twisted as she screamed, fighting a lost cause to save him. Too fucking late; he was already mine by right, and he would feed, I could feel it.

She loved him; it shone from her eyes as she pleaded for him to stop. Those emerald orbs turned on me as she shook her head. "Bastard! You bastard, he was all I had left!" she screamed as a sob racked through her body. My wolf warred with the vampire within me as he sensed her distress, needing to end it. Fucking hell, he wanted to protect her already? *Fuck.*

This was the last fucking thing I needed right now. She hadn't cried when the blade had pierced her flesh, she hadn't begged for mercy as many other hunters had. Full grown men had caved the moment the blade kissed their flesh, but this fierce little female had taken it without making a sound until it had cut through the wall of muscle in her chest.

"He'd die without it."

"Because of you! You fed him your blood!" she accused, her body twisting against the ropes as she tried to get free from them.

"Because he turned when we cut him open. He was fatally wounded."

"I will kill you," she hissed vehemently. "I will destroy you all."

"Nae, wee one," I smirked as I watched the fight igniting inside of her, which only called more to the monster I was. "Ye will do as I say, or I will take his head from his shoulders. Ye are my good wee girl, who is goona walk into that stronghold and do me dirty work, or he dies." Her eyes flashed with anger as she hissed.

"I would rather die!" The chains above her creaked as she continued fighting them, needing an outlet for her anger, one she wouldn't get.

"Ye can nae die, ye are immortal, Isa. Ye ken that ye are a monster, just as I am, nae? They tortured ye until ye buried yer wee beastie so deep that nae even she will help when ye are in trouble. Ye betrayed her fer them. Ye allowed them tae make ye into one o' them," I growled as my brogue thickened with emotion. "Ye will do as I tell ye tae, or he will die. Them or him, ye choose now." I sent a silent prayer to the Gods above that she would break easily, and that the monster inside of me would stop clawing to get out, to reach her. Bloody hell, this was a mess.

CHAPTER FOUR

Isadora

I hung in that room for hours as Jesse turned from mortal to immortal. Unable to save him or do anything other than watch as the bloodlust took control as women turned traitor to the vampires were brought into the room to feed his never-ending hunger. Tears slid down my cheeks as I watched my partner, my best friend, losing his humanity as the change took control. It was my worst nightmare, and I was center stage for it.

The noise of him feeding, ripping through flesh, pushed bile to the back of my throat as I was forced to listen to it. I begged the siren to replace my mind, and yet she remained silent. I didn't blame her, not really. I'd pushed her down, terrified of what she could do if she was released, and with enough medication and control, I'd learned to harness her.

I lifted my gaze, staring at Cian through my lashes as he sat in a lounge chair, studying me while I did the same to him. I had to get away from this place, from these creatures, and worst of it all, I had to leave my best friend behind, or kill him as I'd promised to do. He was no longer human, and the laws of the hunters forbid changed creatures from being allowed to live. More than that though, we'd made each other promises, to never leave the other undead.

Cian was the typical vampire royalty, and if I wasn't mistaken, he was one of the rare hybrids of his race. Rumors had reached us about them being born after multiple mistakes occurring, until they'd perfected them. Still, none had ever been discovered, and we'd considered it myth or a fabricated lie to scare us. The gold in his eyes when he was angered or his when his fangs clicked into place was something I'd never seen before. It didn't bode well for me, or anyone who may try to save us. Not that they would, since capture meant death, and they tended to cut the ties rather than risk more lives in a daring rescue.

He lifted from the chair, nodding to his men, who moved towards Jesse, undoing the chains as he growled and snapped at them with his new dental issue running amok. I wanted to murder them all, and somehow, I knew it wouldn't ease the loss of my friend. We'd been friends since I'd punched Bobby in the nose, and I'd protected him, even if it meant letting my inner monster out to play. Friends like Jesse were impossible to come by, and I'd failed him.

The moment I was alone with the vampire, I turned my eyes back to his instead of wallowing over the empty space beside me. His fingers pinched my chin and stared into my eyes. Golden flecks mingled with the darker irises in his eyes.

"Down tae business, sweet siren," he announced before he released my chin to reach above me, freeing my hands from the ropes.

I touched the ground, but instead of landing on my feet, I swayed on them until he picked me up, as if I was nothing but a doll. He carried me to the chair that he'd sat upon moments before, cradling me in his lap. I swallowed down the rage that pulsed through me as the weakness of my body made it abundantly clear that I had nothing left to fight him with.

"Ye smell like sex and sin," he uttered as he leaned back, pulling me with him as his hand pushed my silver hair away from my face.

"You smell like death," I lied and flinched as his hand stalled, and his mouth curved into a smile. I pushed him down, needing distance between us as I struggled to gain control of my thoughts. I could feel his inhuman heat as it singed my cold flesh. I whimpered as pain flitted through me at the subtle motion.

"I smell like ye, wee one," he uttered as he pushed me down, knowing I had no fight left in me. His body straddled mine as he stared at me, watching every emotion that flooded through me with the precariousness of the position I was in. "Why would ye let them do such things tae ye?" he asked as he studied me. "Sirens are sexual creatures, and yet I can smell yer untried flesh, which means ye have suffered tae keep it that way tae please them. Ye are a virgin," he said as he bent his dark head and rested his forehead against mine. "What did they do tae ye, wee lass?"

"Nothing," I growled. "I did it, knowing the moment she was freed, she would destroy people. She craves death, and demands things that make my skin crawl."

"Nae, sirens are nae truly evil unless ye break their hearts or take something they 'ave claimed tae be theirs," he chuckled. "Older ones, aye, they were the scourge o' mon and women alike. They would pull men from ships into the drink, drowning them as they fucked them. It was nae a bad death, but brutal. It's a different world now, ye ken? It is nae one where ye can lure sailors into the drink and feed from them. That is part o' how they died oot. The other is their inability tae accept that the world changed around them." He stood up, pulling me with him as he reached over the chair, grabbing his shirt.

Silently I allowed him to slip it over my head, inhaling his earthy scent as he dressed me in his oversized shirt. I swallowed as he pulled me up to my feet, lifting me into his arms as I stiffened against his hold. He moved us towards the door, which opened with his magic the moment we neared it, passing through it before it closed again behind us.

Outside of the cell, the hallways were darkened, walls of earth and thick rock mirrored throughout it until he started up a winding staircase. We were deep beneath the ground, and the dimly lit sub-terrain of the structure made it bone-chillingly cold. I folded my body against his, letting his heat warm me as he moved us deeper into the dungeon-like building.

"Where are you taking me?" I whispered against his neck, swallowing past the coppery taste of him still coating it.

"Tae my room, Isa," he replied huskily. "Day is coming, and we will need rest before I allow ye tae leave tae do as I need ye tae."

"I prefer the chains of the cell to your room."

"Afraid tae be alone with me?" he asked as his chest shook, as if he was trying to suppress a laugh.

"I'm never afraid," I lied. I was terrified, because if the siren awoke in his room, I could end up in a very precarious situation that I didn't want. She had a mind of her own, and I'd missed picking up my medication yesterday from the compound, which meant I was two days behind on it, and she'd already taken control of me once around him.

"If ye are nae afraid, why are ye trembling?" he countered as he turned, moving down yet another maze of hallways.

"I'm cold," I admitted.

"I can warm ye up, wee Isa."

"If you mean to set me on fire, fine. Anything else, I'm not interested, asshole."

His dark, husky laughter sent goosebumps spreading over my flesh as he paused at a door, pressed a fang against his thumb, and held it to the mechanism that sat above the doorknob. Great, because that would be easy enough to escape from, right?

Inside, the room was dark and reeked of his alluring scent. A large bed sat in the middle of the wide room, covered in thick black curtains. Next to it was a tub, one that beckoned me to it. I reeked of copper from the blood that caked my flesh, even though the wounds had healed thanks to his blood pulsing through my system. He carefully placed me on my feet, and I looked behind us as the door slowly closed, echoing the sound of my freedom slipping away.

"Is this where you scare the shit of me by telling

me how you plan to rape me?" I asked as I put some distance between us.

"Do I look like the type o' mon who has tae force women into my bed?" he asked as he watched me taking in his luxurious room. He had pictures of the moon and Highlands in expensive frames that covered the walls, as if it was his way of seeing out of the darkness. They resembled windows, as if he was perched in the highest room of a castle, staring out into the world, rather than what it was. Some underground stronghold that never let daylight into it. My guess was that we were beneath a castle in the remains of a dungeon they'd taken over.

"There's only one bed," I pointed out as I spun around to look at him.

"Aye, ye did nae think I would let ye loose, did ye? Ye are my prisoner, wee one."

"Suck it," I groaned as I rubbed my hands down my face, rubbing the soreness of my eyes. "What is happening to Jesse?" I swallowed hard as fresh tears burned against the back of my eyes.

"He is sleeping, healing from his change. It is nae a fast process, but what happens tae him depends on ye."

"On me being your spy?" I asked, watching as his lips curved into a wicked smile.

"Among other things, aye. Ye are mine now, Isa. Ye should nae 'ave fucked with me or my people. I kenned who ye were when we tracked ye from that graveyard. Ye are one o' their best hunters. How many o' my people 'ave ye killed?" he asked as he closed the distance between us, reaching around me to turn on the faucet to the curved, cast-iron tub.

"As many as I could," I admitted coldly. "More

when you release me," I laughed as I stared him down. "Ye think ye can take me on, wee hunter?" he asked heatedly, his eyes glowing liquid gold as he stepped close enough that I could feel his heat drifting off his flesh. I swallowed as his muscles tensed, his hands lifting the neckline of the shirt I wore as he shredded it with one easy tug, ripping it down the middle.

"I've put half those bodies into that graveyard ye visit so often, wee hunter. I am the scourge o' yer people. I slaughter them fer fun, tae hear their pain-filled cries as I rip their souls free from their meat-sacks. Ye think you're the deadly one here? I assure ye, I am so much more the killer than ye will ever be."

I exhaled as my arms lifted to cover the blood-stained bra I wore, but his hands were faster, capturing my wrists in one of his large hands as he reached around me, his nose pressing against my throat as he undid the clasp of my bra. I shivered as my insides turned to lava in response to his nearness. What the fuck was wrong with me? He'd just murdered my best friend, and here I was, melting for him as he spoke of murdering my people. His hand slid down my spine, effortlessly flicking his clawed finger to undo the thin straps that held the panties onto my tiny hips.

"Wash the blood off o' yer sweet flesh. I will nae have ye ruining my sheets, hunter."

I turned away from him the moment he stepped back, and slipped into the hot water, gasping as it seared my flesh. He knelt beside the tub, pushing his fingers into the water before he adjusted the temperature and reached into the small chest beside it, dropping rose petals into the water. Once he'd finished, he stood up and moved to the bed, opening the curtain to reveal the mountain of pillows.

"If ye doona begin washing yer flesh, I will help ye do so. I am tired, and need to rest before nightfall comes again."

I reached to the loofah sponge and started scrubbing my flesh raw as he crawled onto the mountain of pillows, watching me bathing in his oversized tub. Plumbing meant that wherever we were, they'd made some modern updates to the facility. Rumors always ran rampant about them being in old, abandoned castles, and yet there were no hives that we'd discovered in any of the remaining ones. I was going to guess that some type of magic warned us away from going deeper and discovering them.

I could feel the coldness of the earth, being so deep in its depths. The room itself showed that the walls had been modernized, concrete with coded panels that made leaving it impossible unless he chose otherwise. There was no bathroom that I could see, other than the tub, but there was a side bar that was set into the wall, carved in the earth and remaining even though walls had been built with the updates.

"You're trying me patience, wee hunter," he growled as his eyes continued to glow as he watched me.

"I don't have a towel," I uttered thickly as I watched him from beneath my lashes.

I felt magic pulsing in the room and turned slowly, watching a towel float towards me. It was suspended in air, too high for me to reach sitting down. Swallowing hard, I lifted from the water, uncaring that he stared at what the Gods had gifted me to wield. I heard the hiss of air that escaped his lungs as I wrapped the towel around me and turned back to face him.

My eyes flared with fear as he lifted from the bed, staring at me as if he'd found a decadent meal he planned to savor slowly. He reached for my hands, smiling as I cried out as the towel dropped to the floor with his action. His hand wrapped the length of rope around my wrist as I watched him, lifting my eyes to hold his as I stood before him, naked.

Once he'd finished, he bent down entirely too close to the apex of heat that clenched with his nearness. I watched his bowed, dark head as he picked up the towel, drying my legs with detached movements, or so I thought until his mouth touched the inside of my thigh.

A moan escaped my lungs before I could prevent it, and his mouth curved into a smile as he rose to his feet, watching me through his liquid amber stare. He dried off my body, staring at me as his knuckles skimmed my flesh as he slowly, methodically walked me backwards towards the bed. My breathing grew labored as my knees touched the bed and buckled as I fell back. Instead of following me down, he stared at me with wicked heat that burned in his sinful eyes.

"Climb up tae the pillows, and hold yer hands above yer head, bonnie wee lass," he uttered hoarsely.

I climbed up to the head of the bed and leaned against the pillows, watching as he hooked his fingers through his jeans and pulled them down, exposing a thick cock that hung limply against a nest of black curls. It took effort to rip my gaze from that thing to the ceiling as his dark, amused laughter filled the room. The sound of drawers opening and closing filled the room before a pressure against the mattress forced my eyes back to what was happening. He reached above me, grazing his chest against my hard, pebbled nipple as he secured the rope to a hook that he locked before he moved lips against my ear.

"If ye try tae harm me while I sleep, I will rip yer fucking throat oot, pretty girl," he warned as he pulled back and moved further down the mattress of silk sheets. His mouth lowered to the sensitive flesh on the inside of my thigh as I stared at him. His tongue flicked against my flesh, and I bit down on my tongue as his fangs extended. My scream filled the room as he pushed them through my flesh, and pain filled my mind. It lasted all of two seconds before pleasure replaced it, and I moaned as I relaxed into his bite.

My core heated with arousal as he pulled from my blood, igniting a flame or burning hunger that filled my mind as I lifted my need to him, silently begging him to devour me whole. Arousal rushed to my pussy, the need to be filled consumed my mind, and as quickly as it started, it stopped as his tongue slid over the wounds, sealing it.

"Sleep," he chuckled as he moved up the bed, staring at me as I struggled to calm the need that still pulsed through me. Aftershocks of need sent trembles through my body, and I held my eyes closed tightly, unwilling to see the victory I knew shone from his heated stare. "It's a shame we were born tae be enemies, wee hunter. Ye taste good enough tae fuck, this pretty flower weeps tae be filled by me." His hand slid over my belly before it stalled, even as my traitorous hips lifted for him. "Maybe after I have used up yer usefulness, I will fill this sweet cunt up."

"I'd rather not," I uttered as tears slipped from my eyes. My lip trembled as I processed what my body had just done for him. I'd responded to my enemy, and my siren had nothing to do with it. I was so screwed, and we both knew it, but where he could admit it, I refused to even acknowledge what I'd done. I was fucked up by nature, taught to control what I was because if I couldn't, I'd be hunted down and killed by those I called family. Yet here I was, coming undone for him, my enemy; the same monster that had turned Jesse into one of them.

"Goodnight, wee Isa," he uttered as he turned over, leaving me to stew in my emotions alone.

CHAPTER FIVE

Something hot pressed against my mouth and I opened to it, moaning as everything inside of me screamed for more. A strange pressure pushed against my flesh, and I groaned, rubbing my need against it as my body heated, burning for whatever had begun to happen. Mouths crushed together, and my arms burned above my head as I opened my eyes, gaining focus of what was happening to my body.

"Oh," I mouthed against his as I struggled to gain control of my emotions.

Golden eyes watched me, the shift of his body just beginning as he crushed his mouth against mine as I cried out. My legs wrapped around him, pushing his cock away from my arousal as I rolled us over, screaming as my arms threatened to pull from the sockets as the rope tightened. I stared down at him, watching as he smirked, his fangs longer than they should be as his claws scraped against my flesh.

"Cian," I whimpered as his erection slid against my slick folds as the sensation increased. I hissed as his thick cock pushed against the nub that sent pleasure humming through me. He ground my hips against him, and I lifted, feeling him as he poised at my entrance, pushing into me until only his thick tip was buried inside my body.

"Ye want me, woman," he uttered hoarsely. "Ye were the one attacking me, nae the o' way around, Isa. Yer a woman who wants a man, and it's as natural as the sun is."

"Never," I hissed as I leaned over, pulling my pussy away from his thickness. "I'd rather fuck a zombie," I laughed huskily as he smiled.

"Ye can tell yourself that all ye want, but this sweet flesh? It woke me up rubbing against my cock, begging tae be filled, wee hunter. Now be a good girl, and kiss me," he growled as his fangs retracted.

I stared down at his lips with unease before I tried to pull away from him. "I don't kiss," I uttered as he let me pull away from him.

"Everyone kisses," he said as he watched me. My eyes lowered to his chest, and a frown covered his mouth. "Isa, you've never been kissed by a man, 'ave ye?" he laughed with disbelief.

"Fuck you," I whispered as I lay back against the pillows, giving him my back.

"You're fucking serious?" he snapped.

"It's none of your business," I growled back as I turned to glare at him.

"Jesus, they made ye think that ye were a fucking monster, and ye let them. What did ye think, that when ye kissed someone ye would consume their fucking soul?"

"We're not friends so what does it even matter to you?" I asked and then frowned as he moved closer, his eyes glowing as he pressed me down against the mattress and smirked. "No, absolutely not happening!"

"Oh, it's happening, lass," he uttered as he hovered above my lips. "Kiss me."

"Absolutely not," I muttered as I licked my suddenly dry lips.

"Ye want oot o' my bed, ye will kiss me, wee hunter," he said huskily, his words thick with lust as he stared down at me.

"I don't even like you," I whispered as I let the heat of his body warm my chilled one.

"Ye doona 'ave tae like someone tae fuck them," he chuckled. "Now kiss me, we 'ave business tae attend tae, today."

"I like business," I said, unsure whose voice had just slipped out of my throat, because it damn sure couldn't have been mine. "We should just do it."

"We should do something, aye," he muttered as his eyes searched mine. "Ye are nae leaving this room until ye…"

I lifted my mouth to his, groaning as my arms burned from being stretched. He growled as he let me control the kiss, not participating until my tongue pushed into the heat of his mouth. His tongue found mine and skillfully curled around it, sucking it into his mouth as he let loose whatever control he had, kissing me until I was moaning beneath him.

His hand slid between our bodies, and I gasped as his fingers found my clitoris as he pulled his mouth from mine. I moaned, rocking my hips as I stared into his liquid gold stare. The sensation was too much; the multitude of emotion that it sent pulsing through me took everything away until my sole purpose was whatever was cresting within me.

"Oh, ye are beautiful, Isa," he growled as he lifted his body, allowing me to stare at his magical fingers. My mouth opened as noises exploded from it, ending only when he claimed it hungrily. His cock pushed through the wetness of my arousal as I fought against the storm that threatened to consume me. He pulled his mouth from mine, watching me as I whimpered and shook my head. "Stop fighting it," he ordered as he sat back, increasing the speed of his fingers as he smiled down at me. His cock pressed against the folds, rubbing to replace what his fingers had been doing, and as I opened my mouth, the scream exploded as I trembled violently as the orgasm ripped through me.

"Oh my God," I whimpered as tremors rocked through me.

"Good girl," he uttered thickly as I lifted my head, staring at where his hand stroked his massive erection. I watched him with shocked wonder as he pleasured himself, uncaring that I watched him. He growled as his eyes locked with mine, his muscled bunching in his chest as I opened my mouth to moan only to end up having something warm and salty shoot into it.

I sputtered, gagging as I shook my head to get away from the stuff shooting from his happy whacker. "What the hell, ew!" I gagged as I spit it out, only to have more shot in my eye. "Turn it off! Why would you *do* that?" I demanded as I rolled my face into the pillows, wiping it off against them as he continued laughing, unable to stop even though I was moments away from raging. "You're in my mouth and my eye!" I complained as he laughed harder.

"Isa," he hooted, laughing even harder as I turned and looked at him with one eye held closed tightly as it burned. "I'm sorry."

"You did that on purpose!" I accused. He snorted harder as I fumed. "It's not funny! I don't know if you have some supernatural STDs, you jackass!"

He sat up on his knees as I stared at his cock, which had yet to go down any even though it had just defiled my face. "Next time, I'll make sure it's put where it is supposed tae go."

"And where would that be?" I snorted and then frowned as his fingers slid through my flesh. "No, no, there is no next time. We're enemies, remember? You killed my best friend!"

"I didn't kill him, he is undead."

"No, no, you fucking killed him!"

"I'm not going tae argue the logistics o' what he is now, because his future depends on ye being a good wee thing, and doing what I tell ye tae do. Now, come here so I can wipe the cum off your lips, Isa. Show me how good ye can listen tae me."

I studied him before I started to move, only to wince as my arms burned from straining against the ropes that held me. I watched as he reached up to the hook, uncaring that his cock brushed against my cheek as he undid the clasp that held me to his bed. Pulling them down, I groaned as they ached from misuse.

His thumb brushed over my lips as he watched me. "I'll teach ye how tae swallow, my wee bonnie hunter."

"To swallow? I know how to swallow just fine, thank you!" I hissed as his lips tipped into a sinful smirk as he leaned over, grasping my chin.

"Ye can swallow cock, aye?"

"I'd rather bite yours off, asshole."

"Mmm, I bet ye will scream when I pluck that cherry ye been saving. Did they make ye think ye were a monster, Isa? Is that what they did tae ye? Ye are twenty-four, and never been kissed by a man. I get that ye kissed a girl tae chase her off from yer friend, but ye never tasted sin or man because ye thought ye would harm them. Ye can nae hurt me. I am the one thing ye can nae control with that wee beastie inside of ye. Let me play with her."

"No, no, I don't think so," I growled as I rolled away from him and started to sit up, only to have him move with his inhuman speed as he grabbed the rope and pulled me up to a hook that hung from his ceiling. "Jesus, what the hell? Do you have hooks for hanging up bitches everywhere? What are you, the king of kinks, or can you just not get a girl to hang around unless she is actually freaking hanging around?" I seethed as my toes scraped over the floor.

"You've seen nothing yet, Isa. Now be a good wee lass, and cease talking. I will be back. Ye need tae think aboot what ye are willing tae do tae save Jesse. How far ye will go tae protect him, because his life is now in yer hands. Ye understand me?"

"He's already dead," I whispered as my anger came rushing back. "And so are you, asshole."

"Ye think ye can take me oot, Isa? The only thing ye can do tae me is ride my aching cock. Now don't go anywhere, I will be back soon, my lover."

"Not your lover," I hissed at his back as I watched him dress in jeans and a beat-up band tee. He sat on the edge of the bed, pulling on scuffed-up Doc Martins before he stood back up, moving around the bed to where I hung from his ceiling. He smiled as he leaned over, clasping one nipple as his fangs scraped over the flesh. "I thought you were leaving?" I whimpered as I watched his eyes holding mine as he sank his fangs into the globe of my breast. Twin red lines drained from my white flesh.

"Be a good girl, or I'll tear that sweet cunt up and teach ye what it means tae be fucked by a real monster, sweet lass."

CHAPTER SIX

Cian

I studied my father as he paced in the main room, deep beneath the earth of the once glorious keep that we'd built centuries ago. Now, all that sat above it was a ruined house that mirrored an abandoned mansion. He paused, lifting his copper eyes to mine.

"It's about time ye got ye arse down here. What the hell happened?" he snapped.

"We are nae sure, only that the lasses went oot, and they never came home. More and more 'ave gone missing, and even with the lockdown, they still seem tae vanish."

"I've called the clans tae arms, nothing aboot this is normal. Nae bodies, nae corpses left fer us tae discover. Nae trace o' the wee lasses, and yet their makers feel them still. It means they live, but why would the hunters keep them alive? They've never left vampires alive before, always chose tae murder them and make a show of it."

"Cian and the others, they captured some o' the hunters last night. One, in particular, is of interest, isn't she, Cian?" Lars laughed as he folded his thickly tattooed arms over his chest.

"Ye captured some, and they are alive?" Cameron snapped.

I studied my father for a moment before I nodded my affirmation. "A siren, and a newly made vampire," I announced.

"A *siren*? Ye captured a bloody fucking siren, are ye *daft*, Cian?" he shouted as he set the scotch aside and turned to face me with fierce gold-flecked blue eyes and a red face.

"Aye, a siren with emerald-green eyes who is currently hanging in me room," I laughed darkly. "Hybrids are immune tae the bitches, or did ye forget that?"

"The rest o' the men are nae immune. They're deadly bitches. Why in the bloody hell is it still alive?"

"Because she will be working fer me when I am finished with her," I said with a shrug of my wide shoulders. "I turned her best friend, and if she is as attached as we believe her to be, she will sing fer me, and lure the other hunters tae their deaths."

"A siren can nae be trusted, ever. They have nae loyalty tae anyone but themselves. If she has green eyes, ye ken that she is a royal-bred whore, aye?"

"She is nae a normal siren. She takes medication tae suppress it. When I tortured her, it remained hidden. Have ye ever heard o' that happening with one? Nae," I said when his eyes narrowed. "She had never been kissed either, and thinks it unsafe tae let it oot. I think they made her afraid o' what she is. She has been among them since she was a wee bairn, and I think I ken why. When Queen Flora of the sirens vanished, so tae did her wee lass daughter she was pregnant with," I said pointedly. "What if the hunters are the ones who murdered the queen and kept her bairn? She would be a weapon tae wield at their discretion. The wee lass think's she is a monster."

"Nae thinks, my son. She kens what she is beneath her flesh. I doona ken if they would be that stupid tae think they can wield something that nae man before them could."

"There's something else ye should know aboot the wee siren."

"I'm sure her being here and alive is more than enough, Cian," he grumbled as he poured two fingers of Scotch and started to drink it down.

"She's my mate." I smirked as he choked on the liquid amber and eyed me as if I'd misplaced my brain.

"Nae, nae, it is nae possible. Sirens do nae love. They doona have it in them tae do so."

"I did nae say she loved me; in fact, I'm certain she bloody hates me. I did just murder her best friend, but I did that before I kenned that she was my mate. Her blood, it called tae me. I felt it as I drank from her. The wolf and vampire within me want her, they demand I mark her."

"That can't happen. Ye understand that, aye?"

"I ken it, but they will nae be denied her. I did nae fall prey tae her voice when she wielded it, and her blood, while addicting, didn't change that I am in control still. Sirens only kill what they control, and she will nae control me. I will send her in tae find the lasses, because we have nothing else, but afterwards, she is mine."

"Ye chance her turning on ye," he argued.

"Not if I know that beforehand and plan for it, aye? I'm giving her tae them, and I only need her tae escape them long enough tae let me in."

"It's a slippery slope with those creatures. There is a reason they were prized and then wiped oot. They crave violence and chaos as much as they need air." His eyes searched mine before he shook his head as he wiped off his mouth. "Ye will need tae claim her, and once ye do, ye will nae ever find another mate. It is tae risky, Cian. Ye are the future o' the clan. If ye can nae take a mate, it can be challenged."

"Unless I tame her, and I keep her. She is bonnie, and the fire in her eyes is alluring. Her hair is silver, like Flora's was spun silk that reminds of the moon as it fills the night sky. It would nae be a punishment tae fuck that one."

"And if she turns on ye, Cian, she may need tae be executed. Once they choose a target, they doona stop hunting until one or the other is dead."

"Then she'd die. Sirens are deadly, I give ye that, but so am I. I am the hybrid prince of our people, and nae one has ever beaten me yet. I doona think one wee siren is going tae be big enough tae bring me down. I will feed her my blood a second time before I free her. If she is indeed my mate, she will nae be able tae turn on me, aye? And if it doesn't take, she is still useful. I hold the cards, and she will fall into line tae save the boy she grew up with. Loyalty is a human trait, and she is half-human. Flora mated with a ship captain, which makes her daughter half-human, and that human side of hers, it is strong. She may use medicine tae suppress that wee bitch inside o' her, but her mind is strong. I'm not an idiot; I ken how dangerous my wee mate is. I also ken how strong I am, and that she melts when I taste her."

"If she harms ye, son, I will cut her fucking head off and display it for the world tae see," he growled. "This boy, the one ye changed, they grew up together?"

"Aye, they trained together, lived together, hunted together, and now he is one o' mine. I changed him last night, and he is through the fever already. I used my blood tae speed the change so that she can see he is alive. Hunters take a vow tae destroy one another, but they're closer than most. If she is able tae speak tae him, if she sees that he is still within his mind, she may switch easily. If not, I'll let her ken that I will keep him alive and take him apart, piece by bloody piece until all that remains is his mind."

"Three times, Cian," he uttered as he rubbed his eyes and surveyed the room of our men. "Feed her yer blood three times, and then ye fuck her. She's siren, ye doona assume what would work on another, works on the she-beast."

CHAPTER SEVEN

Isadora

Tears filled my eyes, dropping down my cheeks at the reality of what was happening. Jesse, my best fucking friend, one of the only people who had never cared that I housed a sleeping siren, the same boy I'd defended when he was so utterly defenseless as an abandoned toddler was dead. I'd failed to protect him, to keep him alive no matter the cost. It left a hole in my soul, one that I was doing my best to ignore so that the vampire released me. If he released me, I could bring back reinforcements and get Jesse out of here, even if it was only to bury him.

I teetered on the edge of the bed, my arms burning from the ropes that, no matter what I did, seemed to refuse to release me. I was standing on the tips of my toes, pulling against the rope with everything I had in me as I tried to manipulate it to release me as the door opened. Turning, I locked eyes with Cian, who smiled and closed the door behind him before leaning against it and staring at my naked body.

"Quite the precarious position is nae it?" His deep voice rumbled as I chewed my lip, pretending I was anywhere but here. I felt his power filling the room as he moved deeper into it, standing behind me as I faced the other side of the room. "Unfortunately fer ye, the rope is inescapable, and the more ye struggle, the more it tightens."

His nose rubbed against my thigh as his hands wrapped around them as I tried to back up, off of the bed. His deep growl filled the room, sending sparks up my spine as he held me in place. I spun around, noting my mistake the moment his heated breath fanned against the delicate flesh of my apex. Those hands rested against my waist as he stared up at me with flecks of gold lighting his eyes from within.

I moved to step from the bed, but the moment I did, he lifted me, forcing my pussy to rest a hairsbreadth from his heated lips. Well, shite. I shook my head as I looked up, eyeing the rope that refused to leave the hook that it rested on. I peered down as I watched him licking his lips before that sinful tongue slid through my flesh and I bit my lip to keep from screaming as my core tightened with awareness.

"What the hell are you doing?" I demanded huskily, my voice a mix of pure lust and need.

"Rocking yer world, wee siren," he chuckled huskily as he pushed against my flesh again, watching me as I watched him. My teeth bit into the flesh of my bottom lip until it became too much, too many sensations igniting with the simple motion, and I screamed as my thighs tightened against him. "Mmm, ye taste ready tae be fucked. Are ye ready, sweet girl?"

"No! Put me down," I pleaded as I hung in the air, my flesh flush against his deadly mouth as my arms burned. "My arms are on fire!" I snapped and watched as he lifted his eyes, taking in the rope that had, in fact, tightened until my fingers were turning black from lack of oxygen to them.

He carefully set me back on the bed as he reached up, pulling the rope down as I sagged and whined as my arms ached from trying to get free from it. He effortlessly removed the rope and then rubbed feeling back into my wrists as I watched his large hands doing so.

"Cian, Cian MacCameron, the prince of the MacCameron clan," I uttered. "You're that Cian, aren't you?"

"The monster that hunts the hunters and places them upon the pikes around their strongholds, aye, Isa," he laughed darkly as he watched me shiver with his words. "I am that Cian MacCameron. I'm also the head of the largest pharmaceutical company in the world. Ye and yer hunters, ye think nae one is smart enough tae figure oot who is selling blood tae the smaller corporations that go against me fer market prices. I been watching ye fer months now, sweet lass. I ken what ye do when ye are off work, spending countless hours staring oot over the empty graves o' yer people. Only they're nae yours, are they? Ye remind yourself every night why ye are needed, why ye have tae fight us. How many of *yer* people are in that graveyard?"

"One," I uttered as I looked up into his eyes. "My mother is there because she was raped and almost murdered by you and your people for what she was. She wasn't like other sirens, nor did she lure men to their deaths. Yet she was left to be found on the steps outside the hunters' stronghold. They saved me, her child, and took me in. I have spent my entire life hunting down monsters that prey on those who cannot fight back. I don't care if you are the Pope reborn, I will not help you at the cost of the hunters who took me in. Do you know what happens to sirens that are left in the foster system, or any immortal left in one? We become fodder for those who wish to abuse us. I would have been a whore, used to bring men to their knees. Rich men buy sirens to fuck us and to make their enemies meet a gruesome ending. Sirens have only a few abilities that humans wish to use, our cunts, our lungs, or the ability to bring enemies to their knees with one of those two things. They saved me, trained me how to kill monsters, and raised me."

"By teaching ye that what lies inside o' ye is evil? Or by teaching ye that without them, you'd have been abused? It sounds tae me that they made ye fear what ye are, and that they played the hero in yer story. Guilt is a good emotion tae wield against the young ones. Flora was nae murdered by vampires. Those stunning green eyes ye have are the royal line of sirens, Isa. Isadora Kathrine Mihai was her mother, how do ye ken they knew what tae name her wee daughter? Someone in there kenned who she was, and way before ye were born. If they just happened upon her dying corpse, how do ye ken they knew what tae name her wee bairn?"

"You're lying," I snarled as I pushed him away from me.

"Flora Isadora MacPherson was the Queen o' the Sirens. She loved a lad who captained a ship, and even though it was forbidden, she married him. He was the first mortal tae ever hold the title of King o' the Sirens. I ken who she was, because she helped me many times before she wed the lad. Ye are born of a mortal man, and a queen of yer people, Isa. I ken exactly who ye are."

"My mother died after she gave birth to me! I know, because they told me. They told me how she had been almost drained of all of her blood. How she had two rings on her thumb, hers and my fathers. I know because I have them!"

"How hard do ye ken it would be tae kill them both and raise the new princess of the sirens as a hunter? Ye ken how powerful ye can be if ye stopped drinking their fucking tonic that is poisoning ye, aye? Ye come from a bloodline that is purer than my own. Sirens are powerful creatures, once hunted tae be wielded against mortals and immortals because neither was immune. The only weakness a siren has is when she is carrying a bairn. Once she creates one, she will guard it with her very life tae ensure it reaches adulthood, when it can protect itself against men."

"You need to stop lying to me. Tell me what you want from me, not my dead mother."

"I want ye tae ride my fucking cock."

His switch of topic was so fast my brain hiccupped as I blinked and opened my mouth to reply, only to close it as I sputtered. "No," I ground out as I narrowed my eyes on him as he stepped closer.

"Yes," he countered as he took another step closer.

"You need to stop, now," I warned as I held my hands up, only to feel the cold wall behind the globes of my ass cheeks.

"I'm hungry."

"You should try fruit, it's good for you," I offered huskily.

"So is siren flesh."

"Still bitter," I swallowed as I watched him close the distance between us. When he got close, I ducked, slipping around him as I danced free of his hold. I kept walking backwards, staring at his full mouth that curved into a devilish grin before he vanished.

I spun around, searching the room for him and then paused as his lips pressed against my shoulder blade. "Oyo wee, Isa, ye 'ave never hunted anything like me, have ye? Right now ye are wondering how ye couldn't even sense me in the room. Or how the hunters will be able tae fight me," he growled as he spun me around and picked me up, forcing me to wrap my legs around him as he walked us to the bed and sat on it, staring into my eyes. "They can nae fight us, nae anymore. I was fine tae let them take oot the weak ones, or those who hunted mortals gluttonously. Then they fucked with my bloodline, and me wee sister. They will die fer touching one o' my siblings."

"They don't keep them alive," I uttered hoarsely as I felt him growing hard beneath me. "They do not keep them for blood. I've hunted since I was old enough to hold a blade, and never once have we ever been told to bring in one alive."

"Now who is lying?" he whispered as he wrapped his arms around my waist, holding me against him as our hearts thundered to the heady aphrodisiac of the blood that rushed through us. "I watched ye take in a young vampire two weeks ago. Ye and Jesse took him tae the research center and left him with a man wearing a ring with an emblem of a Falcon on it. Who was he?"

"I don't know, above my pay grade. That wasn't a vampire. That was a boy who had been bitten by a lycanthrope creature. He was gnawed on, and yet still breathing. He was different, as if he was somehow avoiding the change from human to wolf. Not vampire," I swallowed hard as I watched his eyes narrowing as I whispered the truth.

"And the young woman that Jesse dropped off three days ago alone?"

"What?" I whispered thickly as I stared down at where his jeans rubbed against my opening.

"Jesse left ye home alone, sleeping. I know because I was inside yer bedroom, watching ye as I waited for him tae return. I could 'ave taken ye then, but it wasn't my purpose. Instead, I left ye there, sleeping in yer pretty blue nightgown as I hunted him down. He captured a young vampire, newly turned at best. He took her to that man again, and then slipped back into yer lousy little apartment, and I watched him, staring at ye as ye slept. Guilt oozed oot o' his pores. So ye tell me, what would make yer best friend feel guilty enough tae watch ye sleep?"

"That isn't true," I challenged as I stared him down. "We don't go out alone, ever. Hunters are always in pairs. Always, it is the first rule of hunting."

"Yer wee baby blue nightgown has a thin layer o' lace ye hand-sewed into the bottom tae add length. The sleeves are nae from the original, but ye are crafty as ye try tae make each measly paycheck they send ye stretch. Ye have millions of dollars hidden in accounts that ye mother left ye, and yet they have yet tae tell ye as much, is that nae curious tae ye?"

"Or they don't know it because she died," I growled as he opened his mouth to argue, and I did the only thing I could to make him stop talking. I kissed him, pushing my lips against his as my eyes widened and I pulled back quickly.

"Nae, continue," he chuckled as he let his fingers trail over my side. "This entire time, ye have not asked fer clothes."

"I'm a siren," I shrugged. "I work best naked."

"Ye are a siren, a bloody fucking virgin siren. How old are ye, Isa?"

"You seem to know everything about me, so why don't you tell me?" I countered.

"I ken how old ye are, but I want tae know how old ye think ye are."

"Twenty-four," I said as I tried to pull away, only to have his hands tighten on my flesh.

"Did ye ken that sirens sleep fer five years after they escape their mother's womb? I'm guessing ye are closer tae thirty, yet ye would nae remember the years ye slept. Did ye remember ever being smaller than Jesse? Ye were a lass, and he a boy, even a year younger, ye should 'ave been tiny. Ye mother was delicate, a wee thing. She had silver hair, spun from the moon's rays. Eyes of the greenest emeralds, and a dimple on her left cheek. Ye look just like her, only yer humanity shines where she had none. Nae until she found yer father, who captured her heart."

"Mmm, does this story have a point?"

"I'm going tae take ye tae Jesse, but first, ye will

feed from me."

"I'm a siren, I'm good. I'm way good, no blood needed."

"I wasn't asking," he hissed as he rolled us without warning, staring down at me as he pushed the massive erection against me. "You're fucking beautiful."

"No," I whispered as I swallowed loudly. "I'm mildly passing or some shit. Stop looking at me like you're going to eat me. It's disturbing, and my eye still burns."

He smirked as he leaned down, pressing his mouth against my ear. "Can ye feel me, woman?" he growled.

"It's hard to miss," I admitted, swallowing as my hands pressed against his chest.

"Not my cock," he laughed as he lifted up, studying my face as I fought to remain calm.

"What then? Because I can't think past that thing poking me," I whispered huskily.

He pushed his mouth against mine, never deepening the kiss or even kissing me as I heard his fangs click into place. I shivered as I watched him, hating the idea of drinking his blood again. Last time, last time I hadn't wanted to stop, and the naughty shit that played out in my head during it? So good...er, bad.

Something touched my lip, droplets of it, before he leaned over, kissing me with his blood-covered lips. I moaned as the heady aphrodisiac of it took hold, loosening the hold I'd maintained on my emotions. I brought my hands up, holding him to me as I groaned at the deliciousness of him as he deepened the kiss, allowing me to lie beneath him as he kissed me with an intensity that shocked and disturbed me.

The beating of his heart echoed in my ears, igniting a fire within me that sent heat rushing through me until my heart beat in sync with his, thundering in my ears as he ground his cock against the wetness he created between my thighs. I bit his lip, growling as I struggled to get more, but he pulled back, capturing my hands as he licked the racing pulse against my throat, pushing his fangs deep into it, pain mingling with pleasure as I pleaded for more.

I could hear every pull against my vein, every moan that escaped my throat as the sensation of floating took control as power erupted in the bedroom around us. Our hair rose as something seemed to click into place. His heart sped up, matching mine as I exploded against him, unable to stop it from happening with his fangs buried in my neck, and his heavy cock rubbing against my pussy. He pulled away, closing the wound before he rested his forehead against mine, staring into my soul.

"Do ye feel me, lass?" he uttered thickly, his fangs still bared as the thick lines that marked his change on the brink of happening slid from them and down his face.

"I don't want to," I whispered huskily, tears sliding from my eyes as I stared at him, unable to shake the intensity of how he felt against me. The sound of his heart as it raced with mine, the emotions that danced inside of me as I tried to piece together what he was doing to me.

"Let's get ye showered and dressed. It's time ye went home, before they notice ye are missing."

"They already know," I uttered.

"Nae, nae, we called fer ye," he said as he stood up,

fixing the large cock that pressed against his pants. "We 'ave everything we need tae bring them down, we just chose not tae use it until now."

"Then why do you need me?" I asked as I sat up, ignoring the fact that his eyes heated as they took in the arousal of my flesh.

"Because I want my sister back alive, and if it means sending ye in tae get her, so be it. If ye fail, they die. Ye get one chance tae do it right, or I bring down hell on them and anyone else who stands in my way."

CHAPTER EIGHT

D ressed in someone else's barely-there white shorts and a red camisole, I was chained to Cian, who yanked the chain every few minutes when I would pause to take in the underground city. No wonder we couldn't find the hives; if the others looked like this one, we'd be walking into a slaughter—our own.

It wasn't like anything I'd expected to see in the hive of vampires. Children played as groups, and those I assumed were their parents stood nearby talking. Men and women sat at long tables, laughing or joking until they noticed me chained to Cian, and then angry glares or hisses began. It probably didn't help that I wiggled my brows as we passed, taking in their wide-owlet stares with pride. I'd earned a massive reputation on murdering their kind, and I prided myself on it, even though the reality was, I'd lost Jesse this time.

Which hurt in every way imaginable, and nothing could change that. We paused outside a locked door, and my chain was jerked again, but this time he didn't stop until I was pressed against him. His fingers pinched my chin, forcing my stare to meet his.

"Inside this room is your best friend, Isa. He is nae a monster; he is the same man ye grew up with."

"You killed my best friend," I argued. "I don't care what you say otherwise, Jesse died when you turned him into a monster, like you."

"Ye can make up yer own wee mind then," he laughed as he released me, moving to unlock the door.

My heart raced as it creaked loudly and I was pulled in behind Cian, to a room of darkness that was eerily silent. I could feel the taint of the undead, and the moment the lights turned on, my eyes settled on Jesse, who was sitting in a chair with his leg resting over the other one, just as he had done countless times as we'd watched movies or spoke of our plans for the future together, at home.

He stood up and then winced when I flinched, jumping back against the heat of Cian's body. Jesse didn't speak to me. Instead, he let his gaze drift down my body before they lifted to settle on my face.

"Isa," he uttered thickly, his fangs noticeable as he spoke.

I stared at him, noting the differences that had taken over his features. Black eyes had replaced the dull brown. It happened with newly turned vampires, unable to control their hunger. His hair was thicker, skin utterly flawless and beautiful. Jesse had never been beautiful; rugged, masculine, but not beautiful.

"It's me, Isa," he continued as I simply stared at him with tears streaming down my face. I couldn't stop the pain that sliced through me. The reality of what he was, and that his eyes danced between black and red as the bloodlust fought for control.

"I'm done," I whispered as I stepped backwards, needing to get away from him now. I turned, but Cian held me, turning me back to Jesse, capturing my chin as he forced me to take in the monster who had replaced my best fucking friend. "No, it's not him!" I shouted, and then with inhuman speed, Jesse was there, touching my face. "Stop it!"

"It's me, the same kid who used to follow you everywhere. The one you gave all your sweets to because you thought I was too skinny. Remember, I used to pretend to be hungry so that you'd feed me your food. You always saved the potatoes for me and asked for extra gravy because I loved it. When we moved out of the compound, it was because I needed the space, and yet you followed me because we are a team. Whatever comes, we handle it together. You and me, Isa—you and me," he said, rushing his words together as he grazed his palm over my cheek even though I backed away from him, or tried to, with Cian holding me in his arms. "Whatever comes, whatever happens, it's us against them, remember? This isn't my end, it's a new beginning. I'm still here."

"You died," I whispered harshly. "I watched you die. I watched you murder women as you fed from them. You are not him, because he would never murder women! My best friend fought for the weak, he didn't eat them! My best friend marched for women's rights, he didn't eat them and enjoy it!" I hissed as I dropped to the floor, swiping my leg out as I took both men to the floor effortlessly. I lunged for Jesse, wrapping the chain around him as I bashed his head against the floor.

I'd made him a promise, to never leave him an undead monster. It was something the vampires enjoyed doing to hunters, turning them into what they were so other hunters could hunt their own friends down. I sobbed as I assaulted him, smashing his head against the cement floor until I was ripped off of him and pushed against the wall. I closed my eyes as angry tears slipped from my eyes, my body jerking as the emotion violently shook through me. Cian's forearm held me in place as sobs escaped from me.

"Jesus, Isa," Cian growled as the door opened and men flooded the room. Cian held me against the wall until it was cleared and then once it was, he stepped away from me. His angry stare burned into mine as he struggled to calm his anger as I sank to the floor, placing my head against my knees. "Just because he changed what he is and what he eats, doesn't mean he is nae the same lad who ye loved."

"This is your fault."

"Aye, I changed him into a monster, and gave him a new outlook on life," he agreed as he sat beside me. I turned, staring at him through my lashes without lifting my head.

The room reeked of blood, a pool of it covered the floor, and my fingers bit into the flesh of my knees as I fought against the rage and emotions of killing my best friend. "Is he...did he die?"

"He's already dead," he announced. "Did ye ruin his afterlife? Nae, children born o' my blood are stronger than normal vampires. He will have a hell o' a headache, I'm sure."

"I promised him that I would never leave him turned

or undead. I made a vow to end him before he became one of you," I admitted barely above a whispered breath as my nails bit into my flesh, tearing it as I allowed the pain to soothe me.

"He does nae want tae die now, ye seen that. Ye were being selfish, needing tae fix what ye think ye failed him on. Do nae put that on him, nae without speaking tae him first," he growled huskily as he grabbed my hands, forcing me to stop puncturing my flesh. "I've spent time with him, and he is nae against living as one o' us."

"Says you, of oh so many lies? Do you think I am simpleminded? I assure you, I am not. I hold the highest intelligence of any being in the history of the hunters I have trained with. I am skilled in murder and killing any creature who thinks to slaughter innocent beings. I am not weak, Cian. I am not buying the shit you're selling, so just stop."

"That makes the next part of this a little easier tae stomach," he said as he released my hands as the doors opened. I pushed up off of the floor and stared down the three vampires that entered the room. "They're going tae take ye tae the medical ward and place a device at the back o' yer neck. If ye stray from the plan, I will kill ye with a click of the button that controls the device attached tae yer spine. Be a good girl, and don't fight it."

"You're insane!" I growled as I watched the vampires closing in around me.

"Nae, nae insane," he hissed. "I will nae allow them tae rape our women, or tae experiment on them. Yer people have my wee sister, and one way or another, I will get her back. Take her."

CHAPTER NINE

Cian

I watched her eyes flaring with horror as my words registered, and then with determination as she moved into a fighting stance, planning to fight off the men, even though she was outnumbered and bound. Her nostrils flared as her green eyes burned, and even as her panic ignited, the siren within her slept. Three punches deftly found their target, her tiny foot kicked a third, and then James locked her into a bear hug as Liam pushed the sedative into her neck.

She was a wee fighter, one who wasn't afraid to die for what she thought was right. I watched as they brought in the gurney and placed her onto it. For all her faults, she made up for it with fire and loyalty.

"I want her blood tested," I said as we started down the back corridor. "I want tae know what they've been drugging her with. Her blood needs tae be tested against the sample from Flora, the siren monarchy. Once the device has been placed, she is tae be returned tae me room. Her blood is nae tae be tasted by anyone else, ye understand?" I demanded as I stopped them as they opened the operating room doors.

"You need to tell us something?" Lars asked, scratching his dark head as he stared at me.

"She's my mate," I admitted as I pushed her silver hair away from her face and let my knuckle brush against the smoothness of her cheek. I heard their sharp intake of breaths, their genuine uncomfortable emotion as it registered just how fucked I was in their minds. I leaned down, inhaling the unique scent of plumeria that clung to her flesh. Pressing a kiss to her forehead, I pulled back, nodding to the surgeon, who pushed the bed with her on it into the sterile operating room.

"The boy, he wishes to speak to you," Liam said, crossing his heavily tattooed arms over his chest and waiting for orders.

"Bring him into the observation room," I muttered as I started towards it, needing to be sure she survived surgery. The pull to her was strong, too strong to ignore with her blood still rushing through my system. The only way to escape the mating call was to kill her or let it play out and see what came of it.

Inside the observation room, I watched as they stretched her arms out, cuffing them onto the operating table. An oxygen mask was placed over her nose and mouth as others took blood and placed an IV into her arm. Monitors beeped and kept track of her vitals, not that I needed them to feel her heart beating, since mine mirrored hers in perfect harmony.

The door opened behind me, and I heard his hiss exploding from him as he took in the sight of Isadora naked from the waist up as they worked on her.

"What the hell did you do to her?" he demanded.

"Sit down," I growled as I touched the pads of my fingers together and brought them up to my lips as I watched them making quick work of what needed to be done.

"She didn't mean it," he continued.

"Make nae mistake, lad, she meant tae bash ye fucking head into that floor."

"Not as you think she did, she is trying to keep her end of an agreement we made as teenagers. Bloody fucking children that didn't know any better," he argued.

"Sit the fuck down and listen tae me," I snapped and watched as he did as he was told. He was young, emotionally charged with the change rushing through him. He was also in love with my mate, even if he'd never fucking admitted it to himself. "When she is recovered from the surgery, ye are going to tell her everything."

"Everything?" he countered, his black eyes watching me carefully.

"Ye will tell her of what ye have been doing behind her back. How ye 'ave been capturing immortals that the hunters study and dissect them tae learn what their weaknesses are, and whatever else they are doing tae them. Ye will make her need tae go into that place and want tae save them. She is, after all, warrior enough tae escape that hell."

"It will hurt her more than you know, if she knows what I have done."

"How long 'ave ye been in love with her, lad?" I asked, turning my heavy stare to hold his.

His eyes flashed red as he turned away, staring at her as they flipped her onto her stomach to prep her spine for the implant. He shook his head as genuine pain flashed through his emotions, something the wolf scented readily as weakness.

"I'm not in love with Isadora, not like you think. We had no family, only the one we were taken into. Even then, she wouldn't allow anyone to get close to her but me," he explained as I listened, sensing the lie he told even though he didn't realize it as such. "She's my family. Telling her that I have been helping them to collect immortals like her for them to cut them open to see what is inside of them, it will break her apart."

"I'm sending her back tae them. Ye understand that, aye? Fer her tae do what I need, she has tae ken the truth. She has tae ken what she is looking fer, and when she is finished helping me, she will either be mine or dead. That choice is hers tae make."

"You plan to kill her?" he snapped as he stood up, his hands fisted at his sides as he took in my words.

I didn't move, didn't turn my gaze away from where they'd slit her flesh apart to place the tracking device and electrocution mechanism. "She's my mate, the bride my blood chose. If she can nae accept it, I 'ave nae other choice but tae end her life."

"Mates are rare, how can you be certain she is yours?"

"I tasted her twice, and I ken what she is tae me. I will nae allow her tae be used against me. Everything inside of me would die tae keep her safe, and if my enemies discovered her, she would be torn apart tae make a statement. That is something I will nae allow tae happen, nae tae her or tae me. Now, tell me what she is like, what does she like."

"Long walks on sandy beaches that end in the death of anyone who feeds on humans. Basically, her version of a date night is murder with a movie and popcorn afterwards."

"She is more than a hunter, she's a woman. I want tae ken what she craves, what she wants, and ye will help me."

"Isa is beautiful inside and out," he sighed as he sat down, watching as the surgeons worked the device into her spine. "She enjoys corny movies, old ones. Not so much anything new or remade. She loves popcorn and hates sweets. She cries at the end of movies, not because they're sad, but because it's just the end of it. She hates never knowing what else has happened to them, because it is just the end. She is fierce and loyal, unlike anyone else I've ever met or probably ever will. The hunters use her, sending her out to test her limits, even on missions we shouldn't have survived. I've tried to tell her that she is in danger among them, but she won't hear it. Isa needs to believe there is good in the world, and that what she does is making a difference. She visits the cemetery every night, staring at one grave marker that holds no name, only a number. I don't know how she knows it, but I believe it is her father's from what I found."

"Sirens are drawn tae their own bloodline. She may not ken who it is, but she feels a pull tae him if that is indeed who is buried there. What is in the building where ye leave the creatures ye obtain fer the hunters?"

"I don't know, I've never been allowed past the

gates."

"What are their defenses like?" I asked, changing tactics.

"Dogs guard the premises, in the parking lot, or anywhere that has a fence, there will be dogs. Armed men with rings like the man who takes possession of the immortals are on the fingers of the guards. They carry weapons that rapidly fire, better ones than we are issued when we graduate to hunter. Other than that, I can't tell you much. They block us at the door, taking the target from us."

"Ye took my sister, Adelaide tae them," I hissed. "Ye had nae knowledge o' what they would do tae her, and ye handed a wee lass over tae monsters. I should rip yer fucking head from yer shoulders, ye ken that, aye?"

"You and us, Cian, it is war. You turn us and send us back to the hunters, knowing they murder us. We take your people and murder them, but turning them over to whomever these men are? That's not something I enjoyed doing. I hated not telling Isadora what was happening, because she's one of them. It made me see creatures like her in a new light, and handing over your sister, if I hadn't been watched through the entire thing, I would have let her go. She was the first one captured, and those men, they watched our team the entire time, and we knew it. I can't undo what I did, but I can help you fix it."

"Nae, ye can nae help us. She can, though, she is created tae bring men tae their knees."

"What are they putting into her spine?" he asked as panic erupted in his tone.

"A tracking device which also houses an electrocution

mechanism in case she betrays me."

"To kill her?" he asked.

"Nae, but she will nae ken that. She will be told that it can explode, leaving her spine severed. Ye will nae tell her otherwise. When she wakes from this, ye will tell her what ye 'ave done, and ye will tell her everything ye ken aboot it."

"And she will hate me for it."

"Ye ken what ye did was wrong. Ye had one o' the women they planned tae dissect under yer own roof and yet ye still hunted them down like animals. Ye returned tae her every night with a lie ready on yer tongue, and I ken this because I stood in the shadows of her room as ye watched her sleep with guilt oozing from yer pores. Ye brought her tae me, because ye kenned I could save her, Jesse. Ye made me into the bad guy by lying tae her. They told ye tae bring her in, and ye called me with yer location. Don't go getting cold feet on me now. Ye brokered this deal tae protect her, with the promise that ye were made immortal tae never leave her side. I held up my end o' the deal, now ye will hold up yours. She will be captured, and when they take her into that place of death, we will be there tae get her oot. The only way in is tae get someone inside who wants us there. Isa can nae ken that what is inside her spine can be tracked. She needs tae think her life is at stake."

A knock sounded on the two-way mirror, and I narrowed my gaze on the doctor who pushed his finger against the speaker. "I have her results back. She is a 99.9% match to Flora, meaning her human father added basically nothing to her blood. Also, the drugs they administered, they have either burned out, or she has been given a placebo. There's nothing in her system that we didn't administer ourselves. There's a problem, though, the moment I registered her DNA into the system, her results were pinged from multiple people. The council has been notified and is on their way here. Whatever you're planning to do, Cian, do it fast. You have the Queen of the Sirens on my operating table, and they will not be kind about her misuse at our hands."

CHAPTER TEN

Isadora

I awoke to pain that sliced up and down my spine, and as I opened my mouth to scream, something touched over my mouth, holding the scream in as eyes filled with golden flecks stared down at me. I tried to move, and those eyes lifted to someone who spoke next to the bed, and then something was injected into my arm, and I relaxed against the hand that had contained my scream.

I sighed heavily as the pain lessened, and the body against mine scooted beside me, instead of on top of me. I curled into him, stealing his inhuman warmth as a shiver slid through me. I could hear people moving around us, touching me as monitors beeped and the room seemed to go in and out with bouts of darkness as I inhaled the male who held me.

"You smell so good," I muttered, sounding drunk.

"You're drugged, Isa," he chuckled.

"My nose itches," I growled as I tried lifting my hand, only to find it covered in a glove. His lips touched my nose, and I moved it over them, needing it to be rougher to ease the incessant itching. I moaned as he placed his unshaven chin there and the world settled as the itching ceased. "So good," I uttered huskily.

"Ye need tae hold ye bonnie arse still, woman," he growled huskily as his arms tightened around me.

"I could smell you all day long," I whispered as my nose pushed against his throat. He smelled woodsy, the masculinity that oozed from him tickling my senses as I opened my mouth, tasting him to see if he tasted as good as he smelled. I felt him tensing against my hold, his throat bobbing as my lips closed against his heated flesh. "You don't taste like you smell."

"Woman, yer supposed tae be resting and if ye keep tasting me, it will be the last thing ye are doing."

"Maybe you should taste me?" I offered as I closed my eyes and exhaled. "I don't feel right."

"You're drugged, me wee hunter. Ye will feel better soon enough, I promise."

"I want more," I uttered thickly.

"Ye doona need more drugs," he replied.

"More orgasms," I laughed as I lifted my eyes to hold his, noting the black gaze that watched me with heat exuding from them.

"Ye should remember that when ye are nae drugged," he muttered as he watched me as my hand lowered to slide down his naked chest.

His stomach tensed as he watched me slowly exploring the curve of his sleek, well-defined muscles. He allowed it until my hand slipped beneath his sweatpants and wrapped around his massive cock that was ready to be used. His jaw flinched, pulsing as I slowly worked his silken flesh as my eyes closed. His heavy breathing was the only indication that he was aware of what I was doing, and then when I started to move faster, his other hand captured mine and held it still.

"Sweet, Isa, yer on heavy pain medication designed to tranquilize horses. Ye are nae aware of what ye are doing. I want ye, ye ken that. I doona want ye drugged when I fuck that sweet cunt. I want ye aware o' who made ye into a woman. If ye wish tae ride me cock after ye are off the meds, I won't bloody stop ye."

"Fuck me," I whispered as I leaned closer, claiming his lips as my tongue slid over his extended fang. I felt him shiver as I moaned into his throat, rubbing my body against his as I urged his hand down to my covered flesh. "Cian, I need you."

His hand cupped my sex, and I moaned against his mouth louder, slipping my tongue against his as his fingers slipped through the panties I wore, sliding through the wetness that awaited his touch. He pushed into my body, and I moaned, unsure how to deal with the fullness, or that I somehow knew I wanted, no, needed more.

"Stop being obtuse and fuck me," I whimpered as he added another finger, watching my every emotion as it played out on my face.

His dark, husky laughter rumbled against my flesh. "Soon, but nae like this," he crooned as he withdrew and rubbed my wetness over my clitoris. "When I fuck ye, ye will ken who is owning this sweet cunt. Ye will feel me as I stretch ye full and make ye scream fer me."

"Really, you choose now to be a gentleman?" I groaned as I rolled my eyes and then moaned as his fingers pushed into my sex.

"Ye are full o' sass, wee one," he laughed darkly as his face seemed to grow darker, his fangs longer, if that was even possible.

I could see the change he struggled against, his need to give in to his baser needs, and yet he captured my hand and stopped me from reaching his cock yet again. He pushed me back onto the bed carefully and stared down at me.

"Ye are fucked up on drugs, Isa," he snarled, his mouth filling with fangs as he stared down at me, his hands pushing mine against the mattress as I peered into the most beautiful eyes God had created. The gold flecks mingled in the black of his changing eyes, even as they slowly changed to that of the alpha hybrid he was. "Ye could drive a saint tae sin, lass," he groaned huskily as he knelt between my legs.

His gaze smoldered as he stared at me, my hands captured between his, held against my stomach. His cock strained against his sweatpants, and yet still, he refused me. "I need you," I uttered as he just watched me, writhing, moving against the small contact of his flesh as he held me down.

"Ye are going tae hold verra still, Isa. If ye move, I stop, understand me, wee hunter?" he uttered as he released my hands as I moved one to rub over my breast, as the other moved between my legs, where the ache was building. He pushed down the band of his sweatpants, freeing his cock, and I moaned as I lifted my eyes to his with an uncertainty of why I had thought this a good idea.

"Cian, don't hurt me," I whispered and watched his

eyes narrow as he took in the way I studied him. "Or shoot me in the eye, because that actually hurt."

"I won't hurt ye," he chuckled as he leaned over, tracing my lips with his as he pushed his cock through my wet folds. His hands boxed my head in, holding me prisoner as he devoured my mouth and rubbed his heavy erection until I was moaning as the sensations consumed me, removing any uncertainty I had as he sent me over the cliff with skilled moves, hitting against my pleasure zone with every thrust through my folds. When he tensed and growled against my mouth, I lifted my hands, capturing it as I held him to me and licked his fangs, knowing it sent a pulse of lust and sensation through him. Hot wetness landed on my belly as he lifted his mouth from mine and stared down at me with a victorious smirk on his sinful mouth.

"I guess you're not bad at sex after all," I mused as I frowned as his eyes narrowed and his smile vanished.

"That was nae sex, Isa," he growled as a smile fought to play over his lips.

"Yes, it was. We both finished, isn't that sex?" I sputtered with rage as he made fun of me, thinking I didn't know what sex was. Of all the shit to try on me…

"Isa, darling, who the fuck taught ye aboot sex?" he asked as he rose to his knees and pinched the bridge of his nose.

"No one, I'm an abomination, one who can easily kill from sex, and therefore I am not allowed to know of it, or ever consider trying it, or I will become the hunted."

"Nae wonder ye are so fucked up."

"Get out!" I said as I started to move away from

him, only for him to push my shoulders against the bed. The blush that covered my cheeks was from shame, from years of being told how horrible what slept within me was. I knew it made me naïve about the world, or about men, but it also kept me from becoming curiously aroused, which he seemed to pull out of me in spades.

"Ye are nae an abomination, lass. Ye are what ye were born tae be. That doesn't make ye a monster simply because they say ye are. They are less, nae ye. They are abominations fer ever putting it into that pretty little head o' yours. When I fuck ye, and I will, ye will know you've been fucked. That much I promise ye, sweet girl."

CHAPTER ELEVEN

I stared at the sleeping man beside me, his hand absently stroking my naked waist in his sleep. The entire room was bathed in darkness with a single candle that played with shadows upon the wall. My back no longer ached, and the drugs had left my system, thankfully. The fuzzy memories of what had unfolded both intrigued and bothered me. I'd begged him to fuck me, and he had straight-out refused because I'd been under the influence of drugs. A lesser man would have taken what I offered; hell, with the siren's voice mixing with mine and the drugs, no male would have refused me. He did. He refused me because I would have regretted it. I wasn't sure how to feel about that, or him.

Lifting my hand, I placed it on his chest and listened to his heart as I felt it, matching every beat of my own. I could sense him within me, and it terrified me. I'd heard rumors of being sired from feeding from one vampire too much, but Cian was hybrid, and that was an entirely unknown problem to me. My face inched closer to the sleeping male, inhaling his rich masculine scent of earth and woods that made everything that was woman inside of me take notice of him.

"Ye think it is a good idea tae be smelling me, wee Isa?" he grumbled in a sexy, sleep-thickened tone that had me scooting away from him with wide eyes.

"What did you do to me?" I whispered.

"What do ye mean?" he countered as he lifted up with a heavy-lidded stare that sent my pulse skyrocketing.

"Did you turn me?" I swallowed as the fear of it hit me like a brick upside the head.

"Ye are a siren, ye can nae be turned," he chuckled as he watched me slip from the bed and shake my head. "Get ye wee bonnie arse back here, woman," he uttered thickly.

I shook my head as I walked to the aged bottle of Scotch that sat on the counter of the bar, pouring myself a glass before I tipped it up and inhaled it before coughing violently as it burned its way down my throat.

"Did ye think that I turned ye?" he asked.

"I don't know what is wrong with me, okay? I don't smell strange men, or listen to their hearts pounding to the same beat as my own. I shouldn't feel you at all, and yet I do. So you tell me, Cian, what is wrong with me? If you didn't turn me, then what is wrong with me that I feel you so strongly?"

He paused, staring at me as he rose from the bed and moved to the side bar, pouring another two fingers into my glass before his own. He studied me before he downed it, and his silence disturbed me. I'd never felt an attraction to another person before, which could mean I was way overthinking this, going crazy, or I was destined to be a future stalker of innocent prey. Not that he was innocent and he *would* deserve it after what he'd done, but I'd never even thought about sex before, and since he'd brought me here, it was pretty much all I thought about. I was a horrible person.

"When do you plan to release me?" I asked, needing to move beyond the sensation he created inside of me. I couldn't even fully blame the siren within, because she was silent the entire time I'd begged this man to fuck me.

"Soon," he purred as he set his glass on the smooth surface and stared at me until I began fidgeting with my hands. "What do ye feel, Isa?"

"Insane, I feel insane," I muttered as I moved to the bed, pulling the sheet from it as I wrapped it around me for some resemblance of modesty. I sat on the bed, staring at his naked frame through my lashes.

His body was a mass of sleek, trim sinewy muscles that drew the eye to every curve, every hard edge that bespoke of strength and speed. Tattoos covered his sides, moving up to curve around his shoulders as if they were armor. An upside-down cross sat over his heart, a sign that he'd forgone the right to be seen or viewed as worthy by God. On his back was a double cross, attached to an infinity symbol. It was the Leviathan cross, or Diamond's King cross, which meant balance and protection, while the infinity symbol symbolized the eternal universe. Black hair the color of midnight dusted over his shoulders, loose and unbound as he'd worn it when he'd first captured me. Lower, his powerful thighs tensed as his thick cock rested between them, nestled in black curls. It jerked, and I lifted my eyes to find his sparkled with gold within the obsidian as he tilted his head, studying me back.

"What do ye feel?" he continued as he pulled open a drawer and reached into it, withdrawing sweatpants. He shoved his legs into them and pulled them up as I watched him. "Tell me, Isa, can ye feel me in yer soul? My heart beating with yours? Do ye need tae feel me close tae ye, tae inhale me in tae yer lungs until ye ken me by heart?" he asked as my pulse thundered as his words echoed in my ears.

"Is that what you feel?" I sputtered as my knuckles turned white as my grip on the sheet tightened.

"Put these on," he said as he tossed me a sweatshirt and joggers. "Someone needs tae talk tae ye, lass. Ye need tae keep an open mind when he does."

"I don't want to see Jesse again," I warned as I reached for the clothes and dropped the sheet, giving him my spine as I slipped into the fluorescent pink joggers and tightened them. His hands slipped around me, trapping my arms as he held my shoulder blades, and his hot lips touched against my steady pulse as he placed a surprisingly gentle kiss against it.

"It scares ye, this thing between us, doesn't it, wee hunter?" he asked huskily against my throat.

"I'm a hunter, and you're my prey. I kill things like you to protect the humans from being your food. You are a hunter of my kind; you kill things like me for sport. There's nothing between us."

"Liar," he laughed darkly as his hand moved, touching above my left breast. "I feel ye here, the speed o' yer heart beats faster the moment I touch ye or kiss ye. I sense yer unease, yer need tae do what ye 'ave never done before with a man. That is nae yer siren, Isa. Ye are one and the same; ye are nae separated as ye think ye are. Ye can lie tae yourself if it helps ye sleep better at night, but the reason she does nae help ye is, she's ye, Isadora Kathrine MacPherson. Ye think she is the anger. That moment when ye begin tae lose control on it, but it isn't. Ye are her, and she is ye, lass. Ye can nae separate the two of ye."

I swallowed hard against his words, closing my eyes against the knowledge that it might be true, and yet I feared to believe it. If he was right, it meant I would be hunted down and eliminated by those who had taken me in and raised me. His hands released me, and I turned, staring up at him as he watched me.

"She sleeps because I made damn sure she couldn't feed off of Jesse. She would have, they told me she would hurt him, and that she hungered for mortal men to consume. So I did what was needed to protect him from me. He was my only friend; at least he was, until you murdered him."

He smiled tightly and shrugged. "Here's a free lesson, wee hunter. Nothing is ever what it seems, and until ye ken all the facts, ye should nae lay blame."

I turned away from him, unwilling to let him see the tears of anger that rolled down my cheeks. The hooded sweatshirt swallowed me whole, falling just above my knees as I righted it and turned back to face him.

"Let's go so I can hear more lies," I muttered.

"Lies are often just truths we refuse tae hear fer what they are, facts. I ken ye are stubborn, and that they made ye think ye are a monster o' men, but that boy ye love so much, he made sacrifices fer ye, so try tae hear the truth in his words."

CHAPTER TWELVE

I sat inside a small room that had a layer of glass separating it from the other side; two chairs had been placed in it. It looked like a jail visiting room with the thick glass dividing it. I sat in the chair as Cian had instructed and stared at the small holes that lined the glass. My nerves were on edge, my heart beat intensely as the door opened and a very much alive, unharmed vampire who resembled my very dead best friend walked in and sat in front of me.

We stared at each other without speaking, me taking in his pasty white flesh, his pretty brown eyes that seemed more alive in death than they ever had in life. His hair was pulled into a ponytail that he'd made into a man-bun. I had hated when he did that to his hair, noting that it was anything but manly on him, but now it looked almost normal.

"Isa," he uttered as he drew a pattern onto the smooth table that lined his side of the glass wall. "You about broke my head and scrambled my brains."

"Next time, I'll do it better," I said as I dropped my

eyes to watch his finger as he drew the infinity symbol. Something we did as children, a rinse and repeat joke we'd made.

"I don't doubt that you wouldn't succeed," he smirked, and I caught it in my line of vision, still refusing to lift my gaze to his. "I'm going to tell you why we're here. How we got to this point, and I suspect once you hear me out, you'll never want to speak to me again."

"You are dead," I snorted as I lifted my gaze to hold his. "Jesse is dead, and whatever you are, you're not him. Nothing you say is true, or can be trusted." I drummed my fingers against the table and watched his fingers as they stalled, and then resumed the symbol.

"Six months ago I was called into the elders' private study. You remember, I thought I was being called in for what we'd done to the werewolves who had turned over twenty innocent women. You remember that, right? The blood eagle we did to send a violent message to the other wolves who had escaped capture that night? Instead of being in trouble for what we had done, as I told you I was, I was asked to help them bring in a few immortals. It was young women mostly, a few others who were young men.

"I didn't question it at the time, didn't even think about why I was bringing in vampires alive. Then I met Adelaide MacCameron, who told me what would happen if I handed her to the Falcon and his men, as they referred to him. I was being watched, Isa. His men had started watching me and studying how I brought the creatures down. I then noticed them watching you. First, they were in the compound, dressed in hunter clothes, blending in with our own, then later again, outside our apartment. I knew something was coming, but I never thought they would do it. My order came in three days before we ended up here. Isadora MacPherson was to be delivered to the Falcon's gate, and I was to walk away and act as if you'd just disappeared."

"You're lying," I whispered as my heart wrenched in my chest.

"You're a siren. You were bound to be sexually active soon, and no matter how much you tried to stop it, or how much shit you took or poison you swallowed, the end of the matter was, you were a creature that would turn. It hadn't been long since I'd taken Adelaide to them, so I reached out to her brother. I took a gamble that he would want her back more than he would us dead. I told him who I was, and what I had done. I told him I knew where she was, but it would cost him. It was a gamble, maybe the wrong one, but I wasn't handing you over to those men to be tortured, or worse, murdered. They promised me that your death would be a quick one, that you wouldn't see it coming. The elder said that if it wasn't me, he'd just send someone else.

"I made a phone call and asked for immortality and for you to be protected against them. I spoke to Cian about what you were, and what they intended to do to you. He agreed that he would turn me, and that you would be safe if we used you to find out if his sister was still alive. You are strong enough to go into that place and survive long enough to open the doors to let the hybrids in. I made the deal for you. I can't protect you if I'm mortal and you're not. They intended to kill you, and that wasn't something I could live with. Cian made the call through the number I gave him. He fed you the location of the barn and hive, and I knew you'd take the call. You always do when vampires are involved.

"The wound was needed to see what you knew of what I had been involved with. Turning me was my idea, though, not his. Cian has only ever created a few of us like him. He is hybrid, and his bite creates them as well. I did this to protect you, to protect us. Inside the building that they had me bringing the creatures to, the men there are the actual hunters who pay for us to work under them. We don't even work for the real ones, Isa. We work for rogue hunters that were removed from the other branches because they use children to lure monsters out of the shadows. They also capture pregnant creatures and study their children if they survive birth. When they're old enough or close to becoming powerful, they take them down, place them into a sterile environment where they can be controlled, and then they dissect them to learn what their weaknesses are."

"Fuck you! Fuck you and your lies!" I hissed as I stood up and slammed my hand against the glass, watching as it didn't crack. He stood up, staring down at me as he shook his head and pink tears slipped down his cheeks.

"Your mother was one of the creatures they captured, Isadora. That grave you stand in front of every day? That's your father's. That graveyard you think is full of unmarked heroes is where they bury the monsters they take apart, or the humans who they took out to get to them. It was all a fucking lie. They've been studying you. The shots, the thousands of appointments you've endured as they poke and prod you, it's because they're learning you. You're not the monster, they are. You were a child, one placed into my path that ended up with you being placed into that white room over and over again, as I was questioned about how your mind worked, or why you protected me. My entire life has been about protecting you from them, and I knew…I knew if I told you the truth, you'd never hear it. You thought they were making a difference, when in reality, they only want to figure out how to make humans immortal like the creatures they have in that building."

"Shut up!" I screamed as I placed my hands over my ears as denial and rage pulsed through me. My power erupted, sending my hair floating into the air around me.

"That bus of children who went missing last year, do you remember that? Remember how enraged you were that the elders forbid you from searching for them? Or how there was no news coverage even though it was an entire bus of orphaned children on their way to the orphanage? You remember how sad you were that they just vanished without a trace and no one else cared but us? We took them, Isa. They are inside the compound even now. I saw one of the boys days before I was given you as a target. I told the elders that you were to be my last mission for the Falcon. He said I would be reassigned to the trial children. Trial children, Isadora! Meaning they injected them with enhanced abilities from the immortals they'd been studying. The boy, he had fangs and had attacked three children already, and as I spoke to the elder in his office, his corpse was brought in as a misfire. They did something to him and created a fucking monster, and then sent him into the compound to see how he responded to being in the population."

"They would never do that! It would endanger

every child there, every hunter!" I snapped as my claws extended and the glow of my eyes reflected in the glass.

"Yes, they would, because they did. Underneath my bed is a safe. The combination is the numbers on your father's grave. Inside of it are pictures I took when they weren't watching me. Every woman I took to them is in those pictures, and every child I could remember from the one news broadcast is there as well. There's a file, my file on you is inside it too. Everything they've ever asked me about you, and asked me to do to you to tempt the siren out of you. They never understood that there was no siren without you. You *are* the siren, Isa. You've always been her. You have been on a placebo this entire time. I know, because I'm the one who has changed the drop-off meds every time. You're not the monster, you've never been one. You never hurt me, not once. Becoming what you are isn't going to change you. You are exactly how you are supposed to be. They believe you're on their meds, so let them. They think the siren slumbers dormant within you, so let them think that. You can enter that building and burn it down. We have to undo what we've done for them, before they create a monster that destroys everything and everyone.

"They're working to make a new race of hunters. One that will not adhere to the laws of the others," he said as he placed his hands against the glass. "Why the hell else would they need children no one would miss, and creatures that should have been kill-on-sight orders that turned into captured orders? When was the last time you were ever sent out to capture a creature, Isa? Never. Hunters don't capture them, we kill. We don't take children and use them to experiment on. That isn't what we signed up to do, is it? Help me take them down. Help me save innocent lives like we used to do together. I need you now!"

I slammed my hands into the glass and watched as it shattered, his eyes flying wide as he stepped backwards. I could feel the magic rushing through me, the power that ignited from within as I let loose the controls I held as I took down the barrier between us.

"Kiss me, Jesse," I whispered in a multi-faceted tone that made his body jerk to do as I bid him to with his weakened newborn mind unable to refuse me. The room exploded with doors opening, and then I was thrown backwards against the wall.

Men pulled a struggling Jesse away as Cian held my throat against the wall, holding it closed from speaking as my anger turned to focus on him.

"Kiss me," I hissed and watched as his lips turned into a sinful grin as his black eyes flecked with gold grew large, spider webs of black seeming to surround them as his own power filled the room, smothering mine as if it was child's play.

"Oh sweet girl, ye doona need tae use that voice tae get me tae kiss ye. There is nothing aboot ye that I would deny, other than ye are nae wanting tae kiss, are ye? Ye seek tae destroy. He is nae who ye want tae kill, is he? He just spoke unfortunate truths that ye cannot swallow yet."

I jumped, wrapping my legs around him as I jerked away, sending him sailing across the room to watch as he caught himself, crouching into a pose to strike against me.

"Ye want tae play, Isa? Let's play," he growled as

he stood up, anticipating my move as I moved to the left, intending to use the wall to escape him before I pounced, only to end up on my back on the cold floor. "You're weak," he purred as he smiled down at me with his fangs elongated, his eyes black with thin black veins that stretched over his face to disappear beneath his shirt. "Fight me," he demanded as I bucked against his hold, unable to dislodge him as he held me down. "Come on, ye can do better than that."

I lifted my mouth, crushing it against his as I rolled us, staring down at him as I lifted my hand, full of razor-sharp claws. He rolled us again, trapping my arms with his as he stared down at me. He rubbed his hardness against me as he watched me.

"Come on, siren, show me what ye got."

I opened my mouth and screamed, sending my song so deep into the room that glass exploded, shattering into tiny shards. The walls cracked as the doorknobs blew off of them, sailing across the room to be embedded in the opposite wall. I didn't stop, I put every emotion and need into it and let the scream of the siren rip from my lungs. His hand pressed over my mouth, and I moaned as I shook against him, unable to stop the tears that broke free as I gazed up at him as he fought to end my life. Darkness fought to pull me into the murky depths, and I let it, knowing that if what Jesse said was true, everything about my life was a lie. I had helped them take out their enemies to pave the way for them to murder innocent babes. I didn't deserve to live, not with their blood on my hands.

CHAPTER THIRTEEN

I awoke to something touching my face, moving it from one side to the other, as if examining it. My eyes pried open, and I stared into obsidian mixed with golden flecks that turned and smiled at me. He stepped back, letting his hand fall to his side as another male stepped into my line of sight.

"Isadora, I am Caspian, Caspian MacCameron. Cian's brother. My friends call me Casp," he said.

"Is that so, Caspian?" I hissed as I tore my eyes from him to watch Cian, who silently gazed at me, his eyes burning with anger.

"Ye are nae in a position tae be a bitch. There's a device attached tae yer spine, and with a simple swipe, I can hit the kill switch. My brother thinks ye can be of use tae us, but I'm nae sure using something vitriol would be wise. Nothing tae say aboot it?" he asked.

"There was no question asked."

"So ye can be a good bitch?"

"Enough," Cian growled.

"Nae, our sister is in the hands o' monsters enduring

God knows what, and this creature is the only chance we 'ave o' getting in tae that building, so if I 'ave tae beat her tae death tae get my point across, ye best believe I will do it, brother."

"Enough, boys," a third voice said, and my eyes shifted to the shadows. "Isadora, there are some verra important things tae discuss."

"I got that part already." I stared at their father, who looked a lot more like Caspian than he did Cian. Caspian had red eyes as he stared at me, which meant he was a vampire, and he needed to eat a Snickers candy bar because he was hangry. Their father smiled, and my gaze drifted back to Cian who stood off to the side, peering at me with heated eyes. "Get to the part where you let me go."

"My name is Cameron, and I am the laird of an entire clan of hybrid creatures. Ye understand what I am saying, Isadora?"

"I'm not slow, Cameron. I'm pissed. There is a huge difference between the two. I understand you want me to go back to the hunters and be captured, so that I can open up some door for you and your men, but what makes you think they won't kill me before I ever get inside that compound?"

"They need the blood that flows from yer veins. Sirens are powerful creatures and with the voice o' a siren, they can control men. They want ye alive tae understand what makes ye tick. Ye might get tortured a bit," he said with a shrug. "I doona intend tae leave ye in there longer than is needed, because my son would like ye back alive."

"There's a problem. I don't believe any of this, or

any of you. You have no proof other than a newly turned hybrid asshat who used to be my best friend before he started pushing up daisies to the tune of his new maker. Not to mention he has a serious dental issue that proves he is no longer alive or to be trusted. Give me proof." Cameron grabbed my neck, hissing as I stared him right in the eye without fear. "You can't scare me, I was raised with humans. I've put corpses back together so that a family could identify the remains. I've ripped spines from monsters to watch as they slowly suffocate to death. I do not fear death, for everything dies, even us. You want me to help you by risking my life? Show me proof. If what is being said is true, I will slaughter them all and bathe in their fucking bone marrow. I will burn them to ashes, but I will not do it without knowing that they deserve it. I'm not asking for a fucking miracle, I'm asking you to show me that I won't be the monster who takes them down. I'm more than willing to be a monster that goes head-to-head against other monsters. Of that, you can be certain."

"Get the safe," Cian said as he moved closer to me, nodding at the men behind me. "If she opens her fucking mouth, snap her neck. If she screams, anyone who isn't hybrid dies. Be a good lass and keep yer bonnie lips closed fer me, darling."

I smirked and then was dropped to the floor as the chains were released. I brought my chained hands down slowly as I rubbed feeling into them as men entered the room with a safe and my overnight bag, dropping both onto a table. I lifted my eyes to Cian and at his nod, I moved closer to it.

"We did nae 'ave the combination, as we never

chanced getting close tae ye as we had surveillance on ye." I studied him for a moment before I moved forward, pushing in the numbers of the grave I'd always been drawn to. With a loud pop, it released as my fingers pulled it open.

Inside were pictures and memory cards. I picked up the pictures, placing them on the table one by one. The first was of me, the date on the back a delivery date and the location of the drop. I set it aside and watched out of the corner of my eye as Cian picked up the smiling photo of me as I flipped Jesse off outside a theatre we'd went to last year. The next was of a golden-eyed woman with jet-black hair, delicate features that reminded me of Cian more than the other men. I wanted to ask if she was hybrid, but having my neck snapped wasn't on my wishlist this week. More and more pictures of women Jesse had captured slipped through my fingers until they turned into children. I stared at one, the familiar freckles making nausea push against the back of my throat.

I set them down and handed Cian the memory chips as he lifted his hand to cup my chin. I pulled away from him, stepping back towards the guards who would take me down if I made one wrong move. I didn't want or need his comfort. I wanted to know what was on the cards. I pointed to them as he watched me.

He took his phone from his pocket, and I watched him use his inhuman speed as he texted a message and then moments later, the door opened, and equipment was brought in. Watching in silence, they brought in a TV, another device, and then Cian knelt in front of the device, pushing the one thumb drive into it. Within seconds, I was on the television in my leathers, with my face hidden by a half-skull mask. Training day, where we gathered the youth into the main courtyard and made them wish to be like us.

"What is this?" Cian asked, his eyes watching me.

I shrugged his question off as I watched Branson stepping up to face off against me with swords. I was wearing leather pants, combat boots, and a tight shirt that exposed my midriff that Branson couldn't seem to look away from. My eyes strayed to the crowd as I heard Jesse cussing behind the camera that he ran. Even the 'me' in the video heard it and looked over at him before I turned to look into the crowd. I got closer to Cian, pushing him out of the way as I scanned the faces in the crowd, noting several men who I didn't recognize. Branson swung his sword, using my distraction to get the advantage and I swung out, easily disarming him as I once again eyed the crowd before I stared into the camera.

"What the hell is up with you? Need me to kick your ass so you can focus?" I asked the camera, and I made a face when he offered me an obscene gesture. "Seriously, you're weird lately. Maybe you should go bang Sarah and see if it helps."

"You're not allowed to speak like that," he hissed barely above his breath.

"What are they going to do, spank me? I may like it," I laughed as I wiggled my brows, and then turned as a vampire was brought out as the dome above us closed to block out the sun. I swallowed as I turned my focus to the men who marched him to his death. "Crime?"

"What does it matter, MacPherson, he's a vampire. It's crime enough."

"It matters to me, so spill it."

"He was discovered in an abandoned house, feeding from a toddler after murdering its entire family."

"So why wasn't he just killed in the field?" I asked as a frown marred my lips.

"Don't ask stupid questions," Jesse growled. "Focus, or you may finally get to feel what it is like to be eaten, whore."

"Fuck you, bitch," I said with a brilliant smile lighting in my eyes. "I'm all for self-discovery, but fangs are a hard limit for me." I flipped him my middle finger as I stepped forward, withdrawing both blades as I moved towards the chained vampire. "Unchain him."

"No fucking way," the guard said in a strangled voice.

"Are you afraid? Don't worry; I'll protect you, Hanson. Your virginity will be safe with me guarding it."

I watched as they started to unchain him; Jesse was there, telling me just to take him out, but that wasn't what the elders wanted. They wanted the kids to see a fight, because he promised them that if they trained enough, they could be like me.

"You know what they want, and taking his head off isn't it. They're watching me."

"You know what happens when you fight, and what they do to you afterwards," he hissed as he pleaded for me to just take the vampire's head and be done with it.

I turned and eyed the camera with sad eyes. "I'm used to it, it doesn't hurt anymore."

"Isa, it hurts me, it hurts me!"

"Isn't that cute?" Hanson chuckled as he pulled off

the last chain to free the starving vampire.

I stepped forward, ignoring Jesse as my eyes captured one of the elders as I nodded to him as I rushed towards the vampire, rolling when he lunged, letting him think I was clumsy as he struck me. He rushed at me again, and I jumped, spinning sideways in midair as I sliced through him, landing and twisting to face him again. He lunged and my swords crisscrossed in front of me, and I watched as he stalled, staring down at his body as it slowly slipped apart. I turned, winking at Jesse as the elders moved into the field with the men in the white jackets behind them. I lifted my blades once more, taking his head. I tossed my blades aside as Jesse backed up. The children were ushered from the stands, and when they'd vanished, it began.

"I didn't change," I whispered.

"You know she enjoys murdering everything. She is a monster, and no matter how hard you try, she comes soon after the kill to continue murdering those who do not deserve it," Drake said as he nodded to the doctors.

The doctors pushed injections into my arms that burned like poison as it raced through my system. A long, round and oval gag was pushed into my throat and secured behind my head. I choked as my body shook with a force I couldn't withstand, my entire system starting to shut down as I drowned in the foam that filled my throat and escaped from my nose. I screamed as tears escaped my eyes until my body could take no more. I fell onto the ground, next to the vampire I'd killed, my punishment for doing what they wanted from me.

"Turn it off, Jesse. Go tend to the children below

in the cells. See that they are fed the remains of the vampire before he grows cold."

The video changed, turning on as he walked through cages that held small humans in them. I swallowed past the pain that hit me as he showed me the truth. He spoke to me, as if he knew what he would do. As if he knew that he would die and that I'd find the video.

"Remember the kids from that bus? Well, I found them, Isa. I wish they'd drowned, or just been eaten," he said as he stopped, picking up a piece of meat from behind the camera and tossing it into a cell. The small boy eyed the food, then lifted dead eyes to Jesse before he lunged. His mouth formed into row after row of deadly fangs as black veins slid through his once beautiful face. "I really wish they'd just drowned and gotten into the next life easier. I know what you would say, that monsters like you don't get into heaven, but I have to believe that someone like you would get in, because if not, what the hell chance would an asshole like me have, huh? You fight for those who can't; you are everything bright in my world, Isa. Your smile is like a fire that literally burns shit down because it's so bright. If this is what mortals do, maybe we don't deserve to gain entrance into heaven. Maybe we belong in hell with the real monsters. I don't want to…" A hand moved, slapping his phone from his hand as it hissed and spit, his phone landing on the camera. Jesse picked it back up, staring at it before he started speaking again, only there was no sound.

"I don't want to go heaven if they won't allow you into it with me. I'd rather be damned to walk beside you in eternal hell, bound to never leave this world as long as

I got to do it at your side, Isadora Kathrine MacPherson. You're my best fucking bitch, my best friend. I'd rather die a mortal death and become a monster like you than be like them any day, because sometimes the monsters aren't the bad people. Sometimes they're the heroes."

Tears streamed down my cheeks as I turned to stare at Jesse, who was hidden in the shadows of the room. He stepped forward, his hands in his pockets as he watched me.

"If the hunters are the good guys, I'd rather be the monster. I'd rather be like you, and fight against them any day. You were never a monster, Isa. You were the only one of us who never strayed from their path, even though they laid it down for you. I didn't lie to you. Cian isn't controlling what I say. He only did what I asked of him, so that I was strong enough to fight beside you, without you having to worry about me being weak with mortality holding me back. I did this so that you could be free, and not worry about me. I also needed to get you away from them, so that I could show you the truth."

I shook my head as I remained silent, uncertain if I even could speak. Why the hell hadn't he just started with that video to begin with? It would have made everything so much easier.

"You'd have stopped me," he said as I stared him down. "I knew what I was doing, knew I was able to change without any ill side-effects because my mother was able to be turned. If I had told you that I would ask a hybrid to sire me, you'd have slapped me silly, and you know it."

I flipped him off and shook my head. My hands

moved in sign language as he watched them then lifted them.

"You don't hate me; you're just pissed off because I did something behind your back. You wouldn't have let me do this, admit it. Had I told you that I was going to betray the hunters, you'd have lost your mind. You wouldn't have told them, or even warned them, but you would have tried to stop me. It's who you are. So I did this, and I made sure you came with me. I needed you safe, protected, and unreachable from their grasp as I endured the change. I also know that they intend to take you into that building and breed you, because it is the only thing that makes sense. They're bringing in toddlers, a lot of them, Isa. They won't kill you, because they want you to sire an army of sirens they can control as they think they have done to you. I found records in the basement, and I know beyond a doubt they're raping those women I gave them. They're unable to control the children they injected with the mutations, and all but a very few of them have been put down. Now they seek women, women who can ovulate and have their eggs removed and placed into other women they have captured. Mortal women, Isa. That entire facility is being used to breed babes from other castes or breeds. Think about this. I've captured a hybrid vampire, three born vampires, seven werewolves, two Fae, and nine succubi, and my last assignment was to be you. The last known siren alive. The men are incubi, lycans, and three born vampires. I secured copious amounts of ovulation drugs and stimulants to keep them fucking into the next century. I did that, and now I'm asking you, my best fucking friend, to help me fix my mess."

I eyed Cian, he nodded, and I turned back to Jesse. "You're a fucking idiot, bitch."

"I love you too, hooker."

"No, no, you don't get to say that right now. I'm pissed at you! You died, you asshole! I tried to smash your fucking head in! I'm pissed. You died," I sobbed as he moved closer, pulling me against him.

"Told you, little she-cat, through heaven and hell, we go it together," he said thickly with emotion as he held me tightly.

I slapped him as I wiped off the tears and shoved him away. "Next time, start with the video proof and work up to the part where you die. You made me watch it!"

"No, no, that was Cian's payment for me handing his sister over to the Falcon. I tried to tell him that you'd snap. Jesus, Isa, I'm dead, and you're about to walk into a breeding facility as bait."

"If you had just told me, I'd have set the place on fire and killed them all before we got to the fubar part," I exhaled. "I guess we're doing this, aren't we?"

"Hunters are the bad guys, and the monsters are the good guys."

"I don't much enjoy being called a monster," Cian growled as he stepped closer, noting the way Jesse's hand touched mine. "Hands off, I still doona like ye much," he hissed as he nodded towards the bag. "Jesse, wait with the others while Isa changes, everyone else get oot."

CHAPTER FOURTEEN

I watched Cian as he inspected me slowly, methodically dressing to walk into a trap. I held up the black lace panties and looked at him over the thin, wispy material. "Do you really think it's a good idea to walk into a place where they want to rape and harvest my eggs in a thong?"

"Nae, but I do nae plan tae let those bastards touch ye more than I 'ave tae, Isa. Ye will go in, and when ye can, ye will escape them and open the doors fer me. I will be in tae get ye oot. Ye understand? I do nae like this option, but anything we've done has ended with us still being locked oot of the building. Someone has tae be in it tae let us in. Jesse couldn't get in tae it, he tried, and they almost blew his head off his bloody shoulders. That was the night he met ye in the cemetery, and I had tae clean up the mess he made. I didn't know ye when I agreed tae this. Knowing ye now makes it a lot harder tae send ye in there."

"So before I was just some woman you would send to her death, and now I'm not? What does it matter if I

FOREVER IMMORTAL

come out of there, Cian? I have no life without being a hunter. The entire fabrication of whom and what I was is gone."

"Do ye know what I do fer a living outside of the pharmaceutical company?"

"How would I know that when I don't even know you?" I huffed as I turned around and slipped into the panties, giving him the perfect view of my ass, which he could currently kiss.

"I hunt down rogue immortals. I find the ones who doona obey the code, who feed from the mortals without care, or who abuse them, and I end them. I am nae only the monster the hunters fear, I am one a few others who immortals and monsters fear as well. There are seven o' us, all hybrids who mark and watch our world, and when someone steps oot o' bounds, we hunt."

"That's cool, but I have no plans to stick around here after this is finished."

"Nae? Jesse is bound tae me, and he is nae leaving," he growled.

"Jesse is, but I have no reason to stay here. Why would I?" I asked, turning to stare at him as I wondered why he would want me here, or in his hive.

"Ye can do what ye want tae, Isa. Yer free and a big girl," he snapped as he rubbed his hand down his face. "Ye can stay fer a few days, figure oot what ye plan tae do when this is finished. It will nae be done in days, ye ken that, aye? We will need tae save or put down the wee creatures they created tae, and free the others like ye from them."

"In your bed?" I snorted as I picked up the shirt and slipped it over my head.

"I doona mind, but I can nae promise I will be good, wee Isa."

"See, I wasn't in your bed willingly, and now I'm about to be sent into a place where I won't matter to them any more than I matter to you, Cian. I'm just one of the unlucky girls who drew a short straw and gets to play into the maddening games of other people's messes." I pulled up the jeans and collected my hair, pulling it out of my face as he watched me. I reached into the bag, withdrawing my socks and favorite boots before I knelt down and pushed my feet into them, tying them before I looked back into the bag. "You left my weapons?" I asked.

"Pissing them off before they get ye into the compound is nae a good idea, wee one."

"Or you just didn't trust me in the hive armed?" I countered.

"That tae, ye are a hunter."

"No, not anymore," I laughed coldly as I closed the bag and turned to face him. "Now I'm just one of the many monsters without a purpose who the real hunters will mark for death, because I'm about to slaughter every adult hunter who ever touched me. Everyone who betrayed me or made me think I was evil will pay for it, and afterwards, I may have no soul left to be saved. Maybe I'll deserve what comes for me."

"Ye will nae be hunted, ever. That much I do promise ye, Isa. Ye will be protected by every person and every family whose loved one ye are saving. Ye think we are monsters, but we are run on bloodlines and family. We are nae what ye 'ave been taught, and if ye allow me tae, I will prove it. Stay with me," he uttered as his hand captured mine and pulled me closer as the muscle in his jaw clenched. "Let me show ye who we are before ye leave here."

"If I agree, will you shut up?" I asked as I chewed my lip staring up at him.

"Aye," he smirked as the door opened and he dropped my hand.

"The men are already loading into the vans," Caspian said as he stared me down carefully, an uneasy look filling in his obsidian, gold-flecked eyes. "Ye had a fucked up upbringing, so I can understand yer hatred of what ye doona understand. This is our family, and when someone is missing or in trouble, it does nae matter who or what stands in the way. I'm sorry that I was rough and crass, but she's my wee sister. I can nae stomach tae think of their hands on her, or what they may be doing tae her."

"It's whatever," I said as I stepped closer to Cian until I realized what I had done.

"Have ye told her?" Caspian asked.

"Nae, and ye will nae either, brother. She needs tae focus on opening the door and nothing else."

"Cian, she may nae come back, ye ken that?"

"Awa' an bile yer heid," Cian snapped.

"What?" I asked.

"It means tae leave, and he kens it."

"No, no, I got that part. What aren't you telling me?" I asked.

"I'll tell ye when ye come back here," he promised as his eyes searched mine. "When ye are ready tae hear it. He's a bampot, doona be listening tae him."

"Bampot?" I asked.

"Crazy idiot, ye grew up in the Highlands, and ye doona ken what a bampot is?"

"Uh, no. What century is it from? You're ancient, right?"

He frowned and then watched my mouth as a smile played across my lips before I chewed it to stop it. He was poking fun at his brother, but beneath it, I could sense he was holding something back, and I prayed it wasn't something that may get me killed.

Laird Cameron moved through the hallway, his eyes taking in his sons as he approached me. He stopped, staring me down as if he would say something, then thought better of it and turned to Cian.

"We need tae get moving, they're watching the cemetery fer her now; if she sneaks in, they will nab her."

"We better move," I said to no one in particular, but Cian pulled me into his arms, kissing me until I relaxed and kissed him back before he abruptly pulled away and left me teetering on uneasy feet.

"Now we can go, wee hunter."

I followed behind them until I paused and then started again as Jesse stepped into an easy walk beside me. He didn't speak, even as my hand slipped into his. Whatever came, hell or heaven, we'd go there together. I squeezed his hand, reassuring him that I was okay with whatever happened.

CHAPTER FIFTEEN

Entering the cemetery, knowing I was walking into a trap, sucked. It wasn't the being ambushed part, or even the thought of capture; it was feeling expendable to Cian that caused the lump to form in my throat. I could feel his heartbeat as it matched mine, knew he was close enough that his scent carried upon the breeze that rustled my hair against my neck. I peered up at the brilliantly bright stars that filled the skies above me, noting the illumination of them as the darkness allowed them to shine beautifully.

My gaze dropped, staring at the numbers I knew by heart. The nameless grave that I'd randomly chosen to stand in front of since I'd started coming to this place. It hurt to even consider that this entire time, without knowing it, I'd been drawn to the man who had sired me. To a place filled with victims of mortals and immortals alike, that rogue hunters had slaughtered with my help. I had thought I was making a difference, and while I knew that not everything I had done had been evil, I couldn't help but wonder how many immortals I'd taken out of their way to reach their endgame. I was a pawn they moved, who willingly allowed it to happen.

A twig snapped behind me, and I turned, staring into the thicket not far from where I stood. A bubbling fountain sat mere feet away from me, the camera noticeable in the eye of the angel who played in the water while the smaller one above him spewed it from his mouth. Beside it was a bench, one that I'd often sat on as I reflected over a kill, compartmentalizing what I'd done among the dead who couldn't judge me.

I studied the area, knowing that they expected me to do as much before I shrugged it off and turned back around. High-pitched whistling sounded before pain sliced through my arm. I dropped to my knees, grabbing my shoulder as wetness spread over it. Exhaling, I struggled to get back to my feet as my bloody hand held on to the grave in front of me for balance. It was useless, as poison burned through me as foam filled my mouth. Proof that what Jesse had told me was all true.

Dark shadows with semi-automatic rifles swarmed the cemetery. I was kicked roughly to the ground, the air expelling from my lungs as pain assaulted me. Hands grabbed me, turning me onto my back as I peered up into faces covered in black masks. One male pulled his mask up and stared down at me as if I wasn't a person. Cold, detached eyes studied me as I coughed up foam, foam that numbed and disabled my ability to speak.

The same poison the hunters had used on me countless times before, rendering me helpless to fight against them as they watched me. I couldn't speak, move, or fight back as it coursed through my entire system, rendering me hopeless and unable to do anything other than twinge and twist in white-hot, searing pain.

"Pretty," he laughed as he knelt down, ripping my shirt open as he pulled it from my body. His hand grabbed one breast, squeezing it painfully as he watched my response to him. Another male pushed the gag down my throat as it sealed it off and made it so I couldn't wield my voice after the poison had finished. The male who was openly fondling my breasts grabbed my hair, pulling it as he assisted the man in securing the mask over my mouth. He slipped my arms out of my shirt and handed it off to another man, but not before he wiped the oozing blood from the wound onto it.

"You're a creature of habit, Isadora. You made this too easy. I actually was looking forward to hunting you down and showing you how our division handles weak whores. You really should have stayed missing, but I'm glad you didn't. You see, I called dibs on you." His eyes burned with hatred as they began to glow dimly, telling me he wasn't exactly human either. "I want this shirt cut up and spread throughout the Highlands; if anyone is searching for our dirty little siren, I want them far away from the facility. Hand me your knife," he demanded and in utter silence, unable to move away from him, I listened and flinched as he destroyed my pants, cutting them from my flesh as he nicked the inside of my thigh. His mouth lowered, and he sucked against the blood that trailed from the wound. His fingers slipped over the thin panties and his eyes lifted to mine. "You taste good enough to rape, whore."

I squeezed my eyes closed, feeling my own heart begin to thunder before slowing as he continued nipping at my thigh until his blunt teeth sank into it, causing me to struggle against the gag that held the scream in as my mind tried to shut down what was happening to me. Pain ripped through me as tears filled my eyes. His bite was meant to hurt; unlike Cian's much more thrilling one, his was to inflict damage. As the pain lessened, I opened my eyes and stared up at his bloody mouth as he smiled chillingly down at me.

"I'm going to enjoy hurting you."

I stilled my heart, knowing the wound to my thigh was extensive. I felt the mangled flesh from his blunt, abusive teeth as something else was pushed into the wound as I trembled in pain and watched men stepping up to bathe my clothes in the wound.

"Nothing to say about that? Oh, that's right, you can't talk," he laughed coldly as he nodded to another male, who moved closer with a plastic bag and held it open for everything else. "Burn it, leave no trace that we were here. When I move her, pour gas where she bled, and be sure there's nothing left to show she was ever here," he told the other male, who nodded and stared down at me. Hardon, one of the hunters I'd grown up with, peered down at me with loathing hatred. Anger and betrayal shot through me as I took in the other familiar faces with them.

"You should just kill her for what she did to Jesse. He was one of the good ones. She doesn't deserve to breathe the same air as us after she murdered him." I blinked, confused over his words, but then realized the hunters would have had to say something to get away with this.

"Don't get all emotional. What we have planned for her is worse than death. She will be nothing but a womb and pussy that are used, often. In fact, she's to be my new personal whore."

I blinked at his words, wondering what he'd look like bleeding out. I was roughly picked up, my arms yanked forward as he lifted me, chucking me over his shoulder as his hand slid over my ass.

This is what Cian wanted to happen? He'd allowed me to be sent here, knowing they intended to rape me, breed me, and harvest my eggs to create offspring they could control. Nausea pushed through me as pain twisted in my chest. I didn't know if he was even close to me, or if he could see that the asshole was touching me, defiling me. I couldn't even cry out because the gag was pushing against my throat, preventing me from making sound, and crying, as I had learned long ago, made the pain so much worse than it already was. His fingers grazed the flesh between my thighs and the man next to him grunted, staring at his hand and what he was doing to me.

"You're going to let us watch, right?" the man asked, his eyes black as midnight as his smiled, revealing missing canines. The rest of his teeth looked black in the shadows of the night, but not even the stars dared touch that ugliness with their light. My face hit against his shoulder repeatedly, until I knew it would be bruised. His finger pushed into my center, and I gagged against the mechanism that kept me from throwing up all over him.

"Don't I always?" he chuckled as he withdrew from my body and slapped my ass before rubbing it. My eyes closed as everything inside me succumbed to the poison, knowing that I couldn't fight it forever, or them.

I should have known that the elders would have given them the formula to keep me weakened, to keep me helpless. They'd sent me in to die, and I wasn't sure they understood how zeroed-in this formula was. It literally left me weak for days after it was injected.

It made questions fill my mind, to know what they'd done to me when I'd been oblivious to the world. Unable to register what was happening to me. What if they'd already taken from me what they now wanted? Rage and helplessness was a strange bedfellow. One I loathed and hated with everything within me.

My eyes grew heavy as I stared at the ground, watching the pools of water that reflected the stars. Stars needed the darkness to shine, and it took a shit load of it to make them stand out in the darkened night. My vision blurred as consciousness slipped from me.

CHAPTER SIXTEEN

I awoke to more pain as something pushed through my stomach. I bucked against the hands that held me down and lifted my head, watching as a needle was withdrawn. I was naked, bared to the men who watched the scientist with messy hair and coke-bottle glasses as he pushed the contents into a Petri dish. He tossed the needle aside and then shook his head.

"She is not in heat, we need to start the injections to force her to begin her cycle," he mused as he produced another needle and pushed it into a glass bottle before I was turned and it was pushed into my ass cheek. Several more sharp pricks burned against my derriere before the hands lessened their hold on me. "Place her with the others, and Brad, no fucking her until she has finished ovulating, and her eggs are harvested. We need to push her into it, and as a siren, if she isn't fully in heat, she won't ovulate. I want her eggs as soon as possible to harvest, and then you can play with her as you wish, as long as you are careful."

"Fuck you, I won the right to have her," Brad

snapped angrily.

"Need I remind you that winning her only included having her *after* we'd harvest enough eggs to breed a few of her offspring. The others won't be old enough to do so for some time, which means she will be the only one who can. I need her whole to create as many offspring as Falcon has requested."

"That's bullshit and you know it. I beat the others fair and square to fuck this whore first."

"She's not a whore; in fact, she's never been touched, can't you smell it? Her sweet flesh, untried by man? I have watched this female since the moment she was taken from her mother's womb, and I've studied her on several occasions. There is little about Isadora that I'm not privy to. So while you may have won the right to be the first male who has her, it will be when I say she can be taken. She is, after all, like a daughter to me."

Everything inside of me stilled as I listened to his words. He'd taken me from my mother's womb and studied me? How many times had I woken from the poison to find multiple contusions or pinholes in my flesh? More than I could count, and now I knew why. I turned to look at him, noting the wild black hair and pinprick pupils that studied me before a soft smile played across his tight mouth.

"Good morning, child," he muttered. "I'm sorry you were so roughly handled by the men, but you are quite the warrior, and we couldn't chance you opening that lethal mouth of yours. Brad, secure her with the others so that she is in line for more of the injections, and don't hurt her. I need her body to believe it is safe quickly so that it is ovulating without unneeded stress."

I watched the doctor as he moved to the end of the table and withdrew a light, baby blue gown that he tossed to Brad. "Dress her; her body will lure the mortals to it, and her prized virginity would be wasted among them."

"My pleasure," he growled as he grabbed my arm painfully, pulling me up until I swayed against him. My head dropped to his chest as he pushed my arms through the sleeveless gown, righting it but not before he pinched my nipple until a scream of pain bubbled from deep in my chest. "That will be nothing compared to the pain I will give you as I ruin your face as I fuck you. You don't need to be pretty or whole to ovulate. Are you excited yet, Isadora? I am," he growled as he rubbed his cock against me, and I frowned, noting the lack of it. Compared to Cian, this creature had a tiny prick, which was probably why he got off on hurting women.

I was carried out of the room, into a larger one that had women lined up around the walls, hanging in chains. My eyes widened as I took in the sheer number of them as they lifted inhuman eyes to mine. This was insane. The mass amount of immortal women who hung helplessly made my stomach churn as I watched in silence as others were brought in and chained, as one was pulled down and placed onto a table.

Men in white lab-coats pushed needles into women, while others pushed one down on a bed, placing her feet into stirrups. Her mouth was covered, arms still in chains as they harvested her eggs. I turned, staring at Brad, who had allowed me to watch it unfold.

"You be a nice siren and make that body work so Brad can play with your pussy, Isadora. Ask Hayden, I do play so nice, don't I?" he asked a woman who lifted her disfigured face as my blood turned to ice in my veins. Her eye was missing, and multiple cuts had been stitched back together all across her face. She, unlike the others, didn't wear a gown, but her breasts had been removed and in their place was burned, ruined, charred flesh. "I said, don't I?" he growled as he began punching her in the stomach.

"Brad!" a man growled. "She is ovulating, we don't need her bleeding internally when we harvest the bitch. Afterwards, if you like, you can use her ass again. Her cunt is ruined, still. Be more careful with them, this isn't your personal harem."

"She begged me for it," he shrugged.

"I doubt she begged you to fuck her with a machete. You're lucky you didn't nick her ovaries." I threw up, gagging on it as the mask forced it to stay in my mouth before sliding back down my throat. "She looks familiar."

"She's new, and mine."

"She looks like Flora, doesn't she?" the man asked as he lifted my chin and narrowed his eyes on the gag I wore. "Is this her daughter?"

"This is Isadora, yes. Poor bitch was born here, and she will die here."

"You plan to ruin her too?" he asked.

"No, I plan to kill her once they harvest her eggs. Sirens are nothing but harpies that deserve to be wiped out of existence." He glared at me, turning to the other man as he pointed out another female. "That one has been harvested, right? My dick is hard from this bitch and the scent she gives off. I need to fuck."

I watched them as they walked away, forcing my gaze to take in the other women who watched him with fear banked in their eyes. I turned to look at the girl next to me, her golden stare narrowing as she inhaled and then tilted her head.

"Ye smell like my brother," she hissed as she studied me. "One o' Cian's many women he keeps around tae fuck?" she asked, as if it wasn't some slanderous accusation.

I shook my head, but her intense stare continued even after I looked away. She had jet-black hair and golden eyes just like Cian's. Her mouth was covered in bruises, and her gown was torn and dirty. I could smell the sex oozing off of her. I watched as the men left the room, pulling a vacant-eyed girl with them as the one they'd harvested was placed back into her chains.

"You'll like it here. We get injected with ovulation drugs, beaten if we try tae stop it, and occasionally, we're raped by one o' the many mortals who think they are worthy tae do so. They also feed us, but that is few and far between. Marissa, poor dear, she had the unfortunate luck o' smelling like me brother, so Brad has taken a special interest in her as well. Something about the scent o' the mythical hybrid undoes him. Probably because his wee prick doona get the response he desires from the lasses. So tell me, siren, have ye seen my brother lately, or did ye fuck him tae get his scent all over ya?"

I turned to stare her down as I nodded, wondering how exactly Cian thought this a good idea. I lifted my body, noting the weakness from the poison that still wrecked my system. The door was locked from the outside, which meant I had to get a card to even get out of this room. There were also men outside the door, guarding it with guns. My spine ignited as a shock pulsed through it. I whimpered against the pain as fear sliced through me. Just awesome, he wanted to activate his kill switch *now*?

"You're wired, are nae ye? Is he daft in the belfry?" she hissed as she turned, staring at the werewolf who watched us, mid-shift. "Aye, he'd have tae be daft tae send any lass into this hell."

I nodded as together, we watched the werewolf contorting as her screams of pain caught the attention of the doctor who walked into the room just as a siren began to blare. The lights went out in the building, and I paused, tilting my head. The backup generator kicked in, turning on red overhead lights that made the already creepy as shit place even creepier.

I kicked up, twisting as the men focused on the werewolf, placing both of my feet on the wall. I turned my body upside down as I climbed it, freeing myself from the hook, yet not the restraints. Even that simple action exhausted me, and I leaned against the wall, watching the room as it swam in my vision. Once I could manage to move, I slowly took in the men that had their backs to us. My hands reached up, undoing the mask that covered my throat as I pulled it out, coughing against my elbow as the noise drew unwanted attention.

"Her mouth, cover it!"

"Stop moving," I hissed roughly. When they did as I asked, I took in their weapons and the silencers on the end of them. It wouldn't be completely silent, but it would work. "Point your guns at each other's heads, then pull the trigger." I watched as they fought against my glamour, sweat beading at their brows as they aimed the guns at each other's temples and clicked the trigger as brain matter sprayed the women closest to them. I turned, staring at the doctor who eyed the door. "Give me your card, and the access to the main gates."

"I don't have access," he cried. "I'm a prisoner here too."

"I doubt that," I growled as I moved closer to him. "What is this place, and who are you?"

"My name is Harold, I'm one-third incubus and was captured by the Falcon as I fed from women. I didn't know what was happening until they explained what I was and that I'd been abandoned and left to die by my parents."

"I don't need your full story, nor do I care if you are the victim. What you do to these women is disgusting. Who are these Falcons?"

"Hunters, ones who have been turned or changed during a hunt," he said as a sob exploded from him. "They became better fighters, faster than they were as mortals. The real hunters, they would have murdered them had they discovered they had been turned, so they left and formed their own version, with their own rules. Now, now they are growing more creatures like them to take control of continents."

"By raping and harvesting eggs from immortals?" I asked as I started to release the others slowly, my arms heavy as I undid chain after chain until I stopped in front of the last row. "How do we get out of here?" I asked Adelaide.

Harold answered for her. "You can't, they'll never

allow it. The main entrance is reinforced steel, and you need one of the head guys' irises to open it. The only way you could even have a chance at freedom is if you had an army waiting outside the gates. Even then, there are too many immortals or newly turned creatures inside here to get out."

"But you can show me who I need to kill to retrieve the eye from, to open the gates?" I asked as cramps swirled through my stomach. My spine vibrated again, and I groaned as I placed my hand on it. "Can you, or are you fucking useless, Harold? Because if you're useless, you will just slow us down," I hissed as I pinched the bridge of my nose as Adelaide began helping to free the others as she took in the sweat and paleness of my flesh.

"I can help," he said.

"Do not try to alert anyone for help; I assure you, I will eat your face before it comes. Now give me your card," I said as I nodded at the two vampires who picked up the guns from the floor as others descended on the men, grabbing whatever weapons they could find. I bent down, picking up three grenades that I secured to the neckline of the gown I wore.

"Mom?" a female sobbed as they rushed towards one another. "Are you…" the younger girl, barely old enough to breed, whimpered as she held on to an older version of herself, who stood against her stiffly.

"Nae, ladies," Adelaide groaned. "We need tae escape, nae figure oot if ye crawled oot o' her wee snatch."

I grabbed one of the knives Adelaide held out as we moved to the door, knowing the men on the other side had yet to notice we were freed. They had rushed towards the blaring alarms as the building had gone into a semi-lockdown. I didn't know how Cian had managed it, but he'd tapped into the building's controls. Outside the room, we rushed down empty hallway after hallway until screaming stopped me dead in my tracks. I eyed Harold, who was pushed forward by angry women.

"His eye will work," he announced, and I smirked.

I kicked open the door and the moment I had, gave the order to not move a muscle. Brad had the woman tied up, her face dripping blood as he held the knife midair. I slowly walked towards him, staring at him as fear filled his eyes.

"Hi, Brad, are you excited to play with me?" I asked through a husky tone that slid over him, my glamour pulsing through me. "Take his eye, Marissa. You," I said to one of the other women. "Untie her and help her down. When she is free, and his eye has been secured, show him what being torn apart really feels like."

I watched as Marissa stepped forward, her hand holding a blade as she made quick work of his eye as he screamed in pain. The others watched the doorway, and the moment we had his eye removed, they descended on Twatwaffle Brad, ripping his flesh from his bones with their razor-sharp claws. His wet lungs slurped as Marissa pulled them from his chest and began eating them. I blinked and then shook off the horror of what was happening. That was just disgusting.

"We don't have time to eat him," I grumbled as I moved to where Adelaide stood watching what was happening with a detached look that bordered on humor and boredom.

"So, Cian did send ye in here?"

"You could say that," I muttered as shouts sounded

from the hallway. We hid behind the wall, growing silent as heavy footsteps rushed down it and then headed off in the opposite direction.

"Elaborate," she encouraged.

"He captured me, tortured me, and made me a deal. Here I am, fulfilling that deal," I growled as I turned to look at her.

"Jesus, you're a wee hunter, aye?"

"No, not anymore," I snorted. "Now I'm a just a girl standing in a room, wishing you would shut the fuck up before we end up busted and stuck here, together."

She snorted and stepped out into the hall. "It's all clear," she said before shots sounded behind us. We turned, staring at the bodies that lay scattered on the floor before we turned once more, heading in the direction that would take us to the main door.

In the opulent warehouse entrance, men stood ready, armed with Tasers as we slowly entered the room. My spine buzzed again, which I'd begun to think of as Cian trying to hurry me along or wake me from the drug-induced stupor. Adelaide and I stepped back, allowing the vamps with the guns to step in front of us as they mowed through the men who thought to stop us. I pushed the eye against the device on the gate and watched as it scanned it, turning from red to green as I slammed my hand down on the round knob beside it and watched as it slid open, revealing Cian and an army of half-naked men who were already half turned into their beasts.

"Good girl," he purred as he stretched his neck and then moved his gaze to his sister. "Da is in the car, go. He's waiting fer ye, Adelaide, go now." The moment he said it, he started forward, not even bothering to look at me as he entered the building with his men as they started issuing orders to the women while I watched silently. My gaze searched the crowd and settled on the battered immortals, feeling a sense of pride that I'd helped them escape this hell.

I started helping the women as they loaded onto a blacked-out bus as shots sounded behind me. I turned, noting the small female who had frozen in place at the noise of gunfire and groaned as I moved to grab her, only to hear more shots exploding from closer to us. Something burned my chest. I looked down, watching as the blood spread over the front of the nightgown I wore. My eyes lifted as Cian and his men exited the building, locking stares with him as I dropped to my knees as my air refused to leave my lungs. His eyes widened as he rushed forward, catching sight of the lone gunmen who aimed his gun again. Cian moved so quickly that it took me a moment to relocate him next to the pieces of the shooter before he moved again, catching me as I started to fall to the floor. He hefted me up and loaded us into one of the SUVs, shouting orders before the doors slammed closed and the car jumped forward.

"Nae, nae, Isa, stay with me. Stay with me," he demanded. The car that drove us towards the hive squealed its tires as Cian ripped his wrist open and forced it against my mouth. I shook my head, but he held it to my mouth, forcing the blood into my body as he cradled me to him. "Get us there, now!" he shouted to the men in the front seats, holding me to him as he continually worked my jaw, forcing the blood into my throat. "Ye will nae leave me, Isa. Ye hear me? Ye are mine, ye can nae die now, me wee brave girl."

CHAPTER SEVENTEEN

I stared at Cian from across the room with his blood pulsing through me. Everything inside of me was alert, heightened, even his scent that oozed from me. I'd healed, but that had taken more days than I'd wanted it to. I sat in a room, full of half-breed children they had saved. There were children of every breed, even siren, all looking terrified and unhealthy. I knew exactly how they felt, alone among strangers that would never be their family.

I stood up, noting that Cian's gaze followed me as I moved to the three little siren girls who held hands. All three had silver hair that reached down their backs; skinny, half-starved faces turned to watch me as I approached them. Emerald-green eyes watched me warily as I sat beside them, noting they scooted closer to me, as if drawn by my bloodline. My mother, wherever she had ended up, or if she had died in that place of hell, had created them.

"He stares at you, mistress," one announced off-handedly.

"Does he?" I asked as I lifted my eyes to find him doing just as she had said. In the days I'd spent in the infirmary under the doctor's care, he had remained out of reach, and yet I'd felt him close to me. As if he was giving me room to breathe after what I'd endured. I'd told him and his father every detail, knowing that they were trying to guess at what Adelaide had been put through, but I hadn't included the ugliness of the rape she may have endured. That was her story to tell if she chose to. "My name is Isadora, what is yours?"

"I'm one, she is two, and she is three," she said proudly as my mouth opened and closed and I frowned.

"Those are not names," I winced when they turned sad eyes to me. "How about Katharine, Katrina, and Katarina?"

"Who is who?" she asked with a wicked smile on her lips.

"You choose," I whispered. "Your last name should be MacPherson, like me. I feel you, which means we are sisters. My last name is MacPherson, I am Isadora Katherine MacPherson, and I'm your…um, family." My throat tightened as I felt the prickling of tears at my eyes.

"What is family?" she asked.

"It's the people you choose to be beside you. It isn't always blood that decides that, because blood can abandon you. Family is who comes and sits beside you and says 'I'm here, I am not going anywhere.'"

"Are you going anywhere?" she asked.

"I don't know," I admitted. "I think we should wait and see what happens. There's a lot of you little ones who have no home, and you need one. You deserve the best one, and I'm a little lost, like you right now."

"Because you were a hunter, like them," she said softly as she placed her tiny hand on mine. "We can be lost together, because we are family. I'm here, we're here, and we want to stay with you."

I smiled as I tilted my head, studying her. "For now, you should go get some food before it vanishes. The boys seem to be endless pits that cease to stop shoveling food into their bellies."

"Stupid boys," she giggled as she stood, nodding to the two others who had remained silent as we spoke. Once they'd moved away, I studied them before I felt my heart increasing in speed; turning, I found Cian standing inches away from me as he gazed down on me.

"There are some files we found, some that I think ye should look at," he said as he pushed his hands into his pockets and watched me closely.

I nodded and stood, glancing one more time at the trio of sirens whose blood sang to me. I wasn't sure where our mother had ended up, or if she was even alive, but I had no idea what to do for them. It seemed hopeless; the fifty children we'd saved were either from rape or from harvested eggs, and none of their mothers wanted anything to do with them.

"What happens to them, Cian?" I asked.

"We find them parents," he said firmly as he rubbed his neck. "There's a lot o' immortals who doona have the ability tae create life, so it shouldn't be hard tae find some fer them. Come, Isa," he said, holding out his hand.

I stared at it a moment before I placed mine into his, listening as our hearts connected as one. I could feel his emotions, which I figured was from consuming so much of his blood. My body ached with the slightest touch of our flesh, yet when we touched like this, my insides twisted, and everything seemed to settle into place. It confused me and terrified me that I wanted him as much as I did.

I walked silently beside him, fully aware of the eyes that watched us. It didn't bother me that people stared, it bothered me that their stares were locked onto me, as if at any moment, they thought I would slaughter them all, and worse, I didn't blame them.

In the last few days, I'd noticed them. I saw the way they raised their children together, teaching them to respect humans because, without them, they would cease to be alive. The feeders here were cherished, decked out in designer clothes and diamonds larger than I'd ever seen on even the upper class of Scotland. They laughed, told cheesy jokes, and there was a camaraderie among them that the hunters had never had, which made it hard for me to be around them some days.

We turned into a room, and I narrowed my eyes on his as he smirked. "It's a lot of files, and there's a film," he said with a shrug. "You might as well be comfortable while you go through them with me."

"In your bedroom?" I laughed. "Smooth, Cian," I whispered as I scrunched up my nose as he moved to the side bar and poured us drinks. "And drinks, are you trying to get me drunk to take advantage of me?"

His eyes heated as one side of his mouth lifted. "If I was, would ye run from me?"

"I don't run from anything," I returned huskily.

"Careful, siren," he said as he picked up the glasses

with one hand and the remote with the other, handing me one glass as he proceeded to recline on the bed in a lazy pose.

"When did you get a television in here?" I asked as I moved around to the other side of the bed, setting the glass on the stand as I crawled onto it and leaned against the same headboard I'd been chained to not too long ago.

"When I was trying tae figure oot how tae lure ye into my bed," he muttered as I smiled and crinkled my nose. "This is more horror than romance I fear, so if ye need me tae, I can hold ye, wee Isa."

"I do hate horror movies after living in one," I admitted as I scooted closer, smiling as I sucked my lips between my teeth to hide it. His arm brushed against mine, and as I turned and looked at him, he did the same. "Are you going to turn it on, or were we just going to stare at each other all night, Cian?"

"I wouldn't mind staring at ye all night," he said thickly as he turned, clicking on the television as he deftly maneuvered the remote that had more buttons than I could count on it. I watched him, noting the way the muscle in his jaw clenched as his nostrils flared as my body reacted to his nearness. Men speaking on the television pulled my gaze to it, as I watched Drake holding a tiny, screaming infant. On an operating table sat my mother, her eyes catatonic as she was being sewn up. "That's you," he said as he pushed his hair out of his face. "From what we can tell, they took you from her womb after murdering yer father tae get tae her. He fought them tae protect her in her weakened state o' pregnancy. It is the only time a siren is weak and exposed, and yet they still created ye, Isa. She had tae have loved him, which tae the lore is impossible. Sirens do nae love, they seek tae destroy men. This gives me hope fer us."

"For us?" I asked as I tore my gaze away from the monster that had torn me from my mother to raise me as an experimental weapon. "Why would my parents have anything to do with us, Cian?" I asked as I turned, hiding the fear that filled me at his words as I grabbed the alcohol and downed it in a solid swig.

"Give me yer hand," he instructed as he waited for me to set the glass back down. His hand captured mine and held it against his rapidly beating heart that mirrored mine. "Do ye feel that?" he asked as he pushed my other hand against my chest as he faced me, staring into my eyes. "The matching beats that mirror one another? The need tae feel me when I am nae near. My scent is like a drug tae ye, as yours is tae me. The first time I tasted ye, I felt it. The mating pull that said ye were created tae be my other half."

I didn't say anything because he wasn't wrong. I was addicted to the smell of him, and when I was sexually aroused, it was him I'd wanted to scratch the itch. I felt his heart beating with mine, the need to be close to him, but it terrified me. I'd never needed another person to want me, or crave me. If he walked away, I'd be broken more than I would know how to fix myself, and giving another creature that much power was terrifying.

"Do ye feel me?" he asked, and as I looked up, staring into his eyes, I saw it. He was terrified too; his fear of rejection was there, and I didn't see it so much as I felt it.

"I feel you deeply," I admitted. "Cian, I don't know if I can do this. You scare me."

"Ye scare me tae, wee one. I have never wanted a mate, ever. I always figured it would be something I could just walk away from and nae look back. But ye are nae easy tae do that with. I could nae tell ye before, because ye were my prisoner, then it changed. I could nae stop what was happening tae get Adelaide back. I am still nae the laird o' the MacCamerons. I had tae stand aside and let it play oot, as I was ordered tae do. Now, now yer free and there's nothing stopping me from saying this, Isa. Yer my mate and I want ye. I want tae watch ye hold my wee bairn in yer arms. I want tae be the one who says 'I'm here, and I'm nae going anywhere' fer ye like ye did fer those girls ye hardly even know."

I shook my head as I tried to process his words, and when he opened his mouth, I panicked and kissed him. He laughed darkly as he pulled away from me, ripping his shirt over his head as he watched me doing the same. My heart ached with how hard it hurt, pounding against my ribs as I bared my flesh to him and waited for him to finish stripping.

The moment he backed off the bed, I growled in hunger as the siren within demanded he get his dick back in the bed and give it to me. Still, there was a nervousness that made me tremble at the idea of him being my mate, and us doing this. Rumors stated that if we were blooded, and we sealed the deal, we might as well throw some rings on it because it was the final cherry on the top to the bonding process.

He moved back onto the bed and pushed me down,

watching me through hooded eyes that sparkled obsidian and gold as he gazed down on me. His mouth lowered to my belly, kissing his way down to my thigh as he kissed the speeding pulse there. His tongue pushed through my folds, and my hands dug into the blankets so that I didn't end up floating on the ceiling in pure bliss.

He devoured me, lapping and nicking my flesh with his fangs as he took me to heaven and watched as I floated back down. His fangs pushed into my needy flesh, and I cried out, wrapping my legs around his neck as my hands slid to his silken hair, holding him to me as my entire body trembled as I exploded against his devilish tongue and fangs. His dark laughter made me open my eyes as I realized I'd squeezed them shut. I watched as he untangled my legs, climbing my body until his mouth tasted mine, covered in my arousal and blood as he growled as I rubbed my needy core against him.

"Are ye sure, Isa?" he asked as I stared up at him.

"I am sure that I want this, Cian."

CHAPTER
EIGHTTEEN

At my words, it sank in. Everything I'd ever craved was right here with this man. A family I could create and cherish, love that I knew we could obtain together, and this bond that would be unbreakable. It was within my grasp, and I was going to sink my claws into it and hold on for dear life. I lifted my mouth to his, unable to get enough of him as he caged my head between his arms, kissing me back as if I was his air and he would die without it.

He pushed against my opening, and I stalled as my eyes grew wide as he watched me. He pulled back, staring down at me as he watched me starting to panic beneath him.

"Nae, nae, I doona think so, wee one," he growled as he surged forward, breaking past the proof of my innocence as he growled. "I need this."

"Jesus, why would you *do* that?" I uttered as I moved, unable to accommodate him in my body as it clenched against the invasion. "I think it hurt less in my eye!"

He laughed as he lowered his forehead against mine, staring into my gaze with a heavy, lust-filled one of his own before he rocked his hips. He didn't stop; every thrust was slow and calculated until I was moaning beneath him, rocking with him as he took me over the edge of no return with every move his hips made. His mouth lowered, kissing my throat as he prepared my vein. The moment his fangs slid through my flesh, he started moving in hurried thrusts that left me boneless, helpless to anything other than feel him as he invaded my soul, dominating my pleasure as he took me to the heavens.

My hands lifted to his shoulders, and he captured them, slamming them down against the bed as he withdrew his fangs, licking the wounds before he pulled me up against him, until I was sitting in his lap as he used my hips to control every motion our bodies took together.

"Ye are fucking perfect, and worth the torture it caused my aching cock tae get here," he uttered hoarsely.

"I think I like fucking," I whispered as I leaned closer, pulling on his lip as he groaned as my blunt teeth scraped over it.

"Ye ain't seen nothing yet, lass," he growled as he lifted me, shoving me down onto the bed as he pushed my legs apart and held them against my shoulders as he lunged forward, enjoying the scream that tore from my lips as he let loose his control, sending me over the edge into the blackness as stars burst into my vision.

"Do you know what it takes to see the stars, Cian?" I asked.

"Nae, Isa," he growled as he stiffened, holding me

locked into the endless orgasm as his fingers pinched my clitoris.

"Fucking darkness, a whole lot of it," I groaned as I wrapped my legs around him and rolled on top of him.

I stared down at my mate. My forever immortally-bound mate that would never leave me, never hurt me so long as the bond was never broken, and I smiled. I rocked against him, feeling him already growing erect in my core as he watched me bringing him back to readiness.

"Ye are the stars of my darkness, Isa. The light that feeds my soul. If it had nae been ye, I would still be trapped in it. Unable tae find the beauty who tamed my beast. Ye 'ave him wrapped around yer pretty wee finger," he said as he reached up, kneading my breasts as I moaned and started moving against him. "Come fer me, show me who owns that pretty wee, tight cunt. Come on, siren. Show me how much ye need it."

I stared down between us where our bodies were joined as he released one breast to rub my clit to a steady beat that matched the heartbeats drumming in my ears, together as one. I opened my mouth, screaming as everything inside of me burned, aching for more, for his release to explode inside of me. I bent down, kissing his lips as he used my hips to find his own release, and I groaned as pain burned against the inside of my upper arm. I calmed my labored breathing as I sat up, uncaring that he watched me as I took in the matching marking that he had in the same exact spot. It was an infinity symbol, with three lines through it. Where mine was delicate, his was thicker, more visible.

"What is that?" I asked.

"It's my mating mark," he said thickly as he watched me processing what it meant. "Ye are my wife, Isa. My mate until one o' us nae longer draws breath," he uttered as his eyes glowed with pride.

I leaned over, kissing his mark before I rested against him as I felt him growing ready again. "Again?"

"Are ye sore yet?"

"No."

"Ye are nae leaving this bed until ye are tae sore tae do so, and then even then, I may not let ye up except tae feed ye, wee mate."

"Promise?" I uttered as I lifted, staring down at him with glowing eyes as everything inside of me released, letting the need I felt out, not wanting to hide what I was any longer. I may have been a monster, but I was his monster, and he was mine.

CHAPTER NINETEEN

Five months later at Clan MacCameron Stronghold, Highlands of Scotland.

The celebration for the mating of the hybrid prince of the MacCameron clan was a sight to behold. I paused in the mirror, taking in my growing belly that seemed to get larger every day. Adelaide stared at it as well. The red dress she'd altered for me, since Cian hadn't let me out of his bed for weeks, was snug and exposing the growing child that we'd created. I felt the fear of the weakness, which according to all the books of lore, was normal for a pregnant siren.

"Ye look good, but ye are huge," she uttered as she stared at my reflection.

"Thanks, asshole," I groaned as I stared at the large, perfectly round belly that made this dress look all wrong. I turned, brushing my hair as I ignored the inhuman shape of my changing form. "I'm ready."

"Ye have nae bloody shoes on, Isa," she said as she threw her hands up into the air and then eyed the party that was set up beneath the full blood moon outside. We left the hive for the deeper, more secure countryside of the Highlands, far beyond the death we'd left there. I moved to the balcony, watching as Cian felt me, lifting his eyes to hold mine with love so deep and intense inside of them that it often terrified me.

"I don't need shoes," I said as I headed to the stairs, slowly waddling down them as I forwent the tradition of Cameron walking me to my husband as I threw myself into his arms and planted my lips against his.

"Is she bare-footed?" Cameron asked as someone else cleared their throat.

"Aye, she is," Caspian laughed as he cleared his throat again.

Cian set me down, staring at me as his forehead pressed against mine. "I got ye something," he chuckled.

"I didn't know we were supposed to exchange gifts," I whispered. At my panicked look, he ushered one of his men closer, who barely contained his laughter as he approached. I eyed the box suspiciously as I accepted it, shaking it against my ear as I narrowed my eyes on Cian. It took two seconds to open the box and pull out the pair of goggles. I frowned as I looked up at his lips that shook with laughter. "I don't follow."

"Tae protect your pretty eyes, wee mate," he laughed as my jaw dropped open and then I laughed as everyone else stood around us, not following the joke he'd played on me. "We can try them later, aye?"

"Why would she need goggles?" Cameron asked,

his eyes narrowed as he looked between us before exploding in laughter as the others caught on to the joke as a blush filled my cheeks.

"Ye are beautiful tonight, wife," he growled.

"I'm the size of a house, Cian," I uttered as a pain shot down my spine. I ignored it, even as it wrapped around my middle, but he'd felt it.

"Isa?" he asked, and the sound of vehicles approaching made us both stiffen. Men started moving about as Cian reached down, lifting me, but the yard exploded in power as ancient immortals circled around us.

"Ye could have knocked, ye ken?" Cameron growled as he stepped closer to us. Caspian did the same, even as the tallest of the newcomers looked over his shoulder, directly at me.

"What is the bloody fun of knocking when we make such a commanding entrance?" he mused as he pushed Cameron aside and nodded for Cian to put me down. His green eyes studied me, and I felt a slight pull to him as he watched me and smiled. "Isadora MacPherson, is it?"

"Yes," I answered as another pain shot through me.

"Siren and *human*, I am told?"

"I don't know?" I answered truthfully. "I was told that I am, but I do not have proof of any of it."

"She is both," Cian growled.

"I can smell her, Ian," one of the others said as they neared us, even as I hissed and lowered my chin, assessing the threat around us.

"She has my eyes," he said as he reached forward, pinching my chin as I held perfectly still, glaring at him.

"And my glare, along with a grandchild," he said as he lowered his hand and I hissed as I jumped back, my claws extending as I moved to protect my young. The entire party held their breath as the ancient ones watched us with cold calculation. Ian held up his hand and smiled at me. He stepped closer, holding out his hand with the palm up as I watched him.

"Take my hand, daughter. I will show you that I carry no ill will towards your unborn babe. It will be my first grandchild, and the only young I have been aware of." I swallowed as I heard my own snort. "You see, Flora never told me of you, and I searched for you, but you were hidden from me. I'm guessing someone added something into your system to make sure no siren around you could discover who you were. You are the heir to my throne, the only child I have sired."

"I don't know you."

"And I you, but you are mine. You feel me, Isadora, as I feel you. I didn't know you existed, or I'd have destroyed the world to find you. Your mother, she was selfish, horribly so. She lay with me, procuring a purebred child before she disappeared to marry a human. She wanted my throne, to claim it to merge with hers. She was beautiful, just like you are. Flora held no humanity in her, and her human king was the only thing she ever loved. I tracked her down when the rumors of her pregnancy and the timeline was announced, praying that she carried my young. I never found her, only the scent of her in a graveyard, and then her corpse in a grave in a cemetery full of immortals just like her. I gave up hope that you were alive. I sent men out to look within every corner of the world, but they always came back with no news. I don't know if you knew her, or what happened, but I'm here now. I am your father, Isadora. You're not a MacPherson. You're a Campbell, from the once most powerful sirens to ever grace this world. Unlike the others, they birthed a king, me." His eyes lowered to my belly that I held as pain pushed through it. "Sirens cannot birth male babes. Our clan did, though, and through it, I was created. The most powerful siren to ever live, and you are my daughter."

"Isa," Cian growled as the pain worsened.

"It's time," I uttered as I placed my hand into my father's and waited for his emotions to hit me, and when they did, I felt purity, love, shock, and pride.

I cried out as pain struck again, coming faster and faster as Cian shook his head, as something wet trickled down my legs. He inhaled and turned to his father. "Fetch the doctor; it is coming faster than it should." I was picked up and carried up the stairs, placed back into the bedroom where I'd gotten ready for the event. Cian pulled the dress off, ripping it from me as he helped me into the bed.

Screaming erupted as my body felt as if it was being ripped in half from inside of me. Cian's hand held mine, even as the bones broke as I sat up, bearing down with everything I had as more pain tore through me. I leaned back, noting that he'd sat behind me, cradling me with his body as I pushed.

"You read too many stupid books between sex, jerk-face," I muttered before it happened again and I felt my body pushing, even as the doctor rushed into the room, taking in the situation as he pulled on gloves and knelt between my legs. Tears streamed down my face as he looked up, locking eyes with Cian over my shoulder.

"Isadora, don't push no matter what your body says to do, do not push," he ordered as he untangled something and then exhaled. He looked up and nodded. "Next contraction, push and bring our newest clan member into this world, wee Isa."

"I wanted drugs, lots of drugs. He literally owns a pharmaceutical company, so why aren't there drugs?" I cried as another contraction hit, and I pushed with everything I had, screaming as it felt as if I was being tortured instead of what people called the most beautiful thing ever. Fucking liars, all of those assholes were nothing but liars!

"Good job, momma," he crooned as he pulled a red, squalling golden-eyed babe from my body and placed him on my stomach. I blinked, staring down into his startled gaze as he looked at Cian and me as we took in the somewhat wrinkled perfect baby.

A sob exploded from me as I looked at him; he was perfect, if a little red and squishy. I reached down, pulling him to me as I shook with fear. "Oh my God, we shouldn't do this. I'm not ready yet." I looked up at the doctor whose mouth opened and closed before I felt Cian shaking behind me.

"It's a wee bit late tae change yer mind, my love. He's here."

"So much for that theory of never making boys," I muttered as I stared at my son, cradling him as he looked up at me. "I am so sorry that I'll probably screw this up." I smiled as his finger wrapped around mine, as if he was disagreeing. Tears slipped down my cheek as I watched him, and then watched a steady stream of something shooting over my shoulder, and heard Cian as he sputtered behind me.

"Oh gads, it's in my mouth and my eyes," he gagged.

I reached over, grabbing the goggles that had been discarded on the bed, and handed them to him. I laughed silently as I leaned down, kissing my son on his head as I smiled wickedly as his dad continued to complain about his wee son's aim.

"Maybe we should name him Karma?" I chuckled.

"That's a wee lass's name, not a lad," he grumbled.

Less than an hour later, I was dressed in a soft cotton gown, already healed from birthing my son with the immortality that ran through me when the visitors were allowed in. Jesse came first with my sisters behind him, and all cooed and seemed to think baby talk was what my son would understand, so I didn't argue it.

"Whatever comes," Jesse said as he reached out and ran his finger over the silver curls of my son's head. "Jesus, Isa, you created a baby," he said in disbelief as we stared at one another.

"We face it together," I said with a grin as pride lit his eyes as he took in what I had created.

"As a family," Katherine said as she made a silly face as her nephew stared up at her as if she'd lost her shit.

"May we come in?" Ian asked as Cameron stood behind him, trying to see over his shoulder at his firstborn grandson. Caspian was right at his side. I smiled and nodded, noting that they all looked proud that we'd had sex and made a baby, which to me, felt weird. I held my son out, letting them take in his utter perfection as the pain of his entrance into this world was forgotten, and the plans to make more filled my mind. "Is it a boy?"

"Meet Arius," I whispered. "My darkest star and the light of my night," I said as I kissed his light head.

"It's a good strong name, daughter." He hesitated, and I smiled, lifting my eyes to his as he smiled and then eyed the girls. "Are they yours too?"

"They are my sisters," I admitted. "They're part of my family."

"Then I will welcome them with you when you come to visit your home. Your mother was always selfish, but had I known you existed, I'd have crushed the bastards with my bare hands to save you. Your blood was a match to mine when Cian ran it, and I came as fast as I could. I am sorry that I didn't know sooner that you had been born."

I watched as he nodded and Cian shooed everyone out of the room before he pulled on the goggles and moved back to the bed, smirking as he pointed at them. "This looks hot, admit it, mate," he laughed as he stared down at us, his eyes filling with love as he took in his new family.

"You're a dork, Cian, but I love you."

"I love you tae, Isa, and thank you for my son. He is as perfect as his mother; though he needs tae control that wee thing o' his."

"Good, you can teach him as you learn too."

~The End~

ABOUT THE AUTHOR

Amelia lives in the great Pacific Northwest with her family. When not writing, she can be found on her author page, hanging out with fans, or dreaming up new twisting plots. She's an avid reader of everything paranormal romance.

Stalker links!

Facebook: https://www.facebook.com/authorameliahutchins
Website: http://amelia-hutchins.com/
Amazon: http://www.amazon.com/Amelia-Hutchins/e/B00D5OASEG
Goodreads: https://www.goodreads.com/author/show/7092218.Amelia_Hutchins
Twitter: https://twitter.com/ameliaauthor
Pinterest: http://www.pinterest.com/ameliahutchins
Instagram: https://www.instagram.com/author.amelia.hutchins/
Facebook Author Group: https://goo.gl/BqpCVK

...ree UK Ltd.
...K
...60123
...0001B/32